BABUSHKA!

Grandmother's Bench

by

Barbara S. Johnston

Hats Off Books

BABUSHKA! Grandmother's Bench

Copyright © 2000 Barbara S. Johnston

All Rights Reserved.

No part of this book may be reproduced or retransmitted in any form or by any means without the written permission of the publisher.

Published by Hats Off Books
an imprint of iPublisher, Inc.
For information contact:
iPublisher, Inc.
601 East 1st Street
Tucson, Arizona 85705
www.ipublisher.com

ISBN: 1-58736-006-3

LCCN: 00-108347

Cover design by Alexander Steer

Illustrations by Wade Moore

Book design by Jay Carlis

Printed in the United States of America

ABOUT THE AUTHOR

Barbara Johnston is a woman with a mission—to help ease the burdens of elderly women around the world, women she calls "the gardeners of society."

Born in New Jersey after the Second World War, Barbara was interested in writing from an early age. She often earned extra pocket money by writing epic poems for friends and relatives to commemorate special occasions, anniversaries, birthdays, etc: "Since I had to interview people to incorporate their lives into poems, I developed an interest in their lives as well as in history," she said.

Her work was published early. At 16 Barbara wrote a short story for Redbook magazine: "It was called *The Red Sock*," she recalled, "and was basically about the life of a sock without a mate! It was very sad—it was always being left in the bottom of the drawer and used as a furniture polishing cloth!"

Barbara trained as a nurse and specialized in geriatrics. She spent many long hours talking to elderly patients about their lives, which she found fascinating: "I learned then that while we are here, we should live without regrets, pursuing our dreams and doing for others who need help. The elderly have so much to teach us if we only take the time to listen."

She was inspired to start Gray Doves on an overseas trip: "I saw so many elderly people forced to rely on their meager resources after any kind of national and/or natural catastrophe—floods, earthquakes, war, economic collapse—they were so very vulnerable."

Barbara is a natural nurturer and has raised a family of five children and enjoys the company of her 10 grandchildren. She lives with her husband in Denver, Colorado.

My gratitude extends to many people for the formation of the Babushka book.

For their support and encouragement, my family deserves applause.

For his expertise and commitment, my diligent editor at iPublisher, Jay Carlis, gets a deep bow of respect.

To Wade Moore, for the bench sketches and to talented Alexander Steer in London for his perfect cover design, my admiration for you both.

To all the wonderful Gray Dove members who share their time and energy with the forgotten elderly women around the globe, thank you!

Some of the best things in life happen in the twilight of life.

—Andrew Johnston

Table of Contents

My Bench 1
Natasha 5
Irina 33
Valentina 63
Vera 89
Helena 117
Kristina 141

MY BENCH

A place to sit awhile and dream
Of mem'ries long ago,
Where thoughts propel me back in time,
Where I let my feelings show.

I recall events that warmed my heart,
And some that brought me pain,
Where faces I have loved, though gone,
Are with me once again.

I sit alone, my eyes are closed,
Tears roll down my face,
Both with joy or with an aching heart,
I'm held in God's embrace.

I wish for you, a special place,
Like my bench, 'neath the sky above,
A place that's safe, to face your fears,
A place where you feel loved.

Natasha

The date on the newspaper headline banner read June 9, 1999, but it might have read June 9, 1789, for all that it meant to the woman holding it. Today was her birthday, not that it mattered anymore to anyone; it didn't even matter to her. There was once a time, however, when a birthday *did* mean something to Natasha—a celebration of life, a time for singing, delicious food and, of course, friends and laughter. She wondered if people everywhere celebrated the day of their birth in the same way. Not that it mattered anymore.

Viktor's last birthday had been like that—the apartment was filled with friends from the Conservatory who gathered to celebrate another year with him. Raising their toasts to his health throughout the evening, slapping him on the back, they surrounded him with songs and merriment. Afterwards, helping her clean up, he grabbed her and swung her light body around in a circle, saying, "My darling, your are the world's most perfect hostess. Everyone had a wonderful time and they all love you, but no one could ever love you more than I do." Then he kissed her deeply, passionately, as the heat rose in her body and she fumbled to unbutton his shirt.

Without thinking, her fingers touched her lips as her eyes misted with tears. The memory vanished and once again Natasha thought she had been imagining things. She could not clearly remember her past for some reason, so she shrugged and resumed her duties. Tossing the newspaper into the large steel drum set on wheels behind her, she grabbed the handles and dragged it along behind her. Placing her broom over her right shoulder, she trudged across the busy street. Navigating the cobblestones was difficult with the cumbersome metal drum. Although it had been painted to resemble a trashcan, paint alone could not disguise its identity. This drum, as all the other steel drums used by the sanitation workers, came from a chemical plant near Novgorod, a city in the north. When they were new, they had an odd smell, but her nose had become accustomed to it and her eyes no longer itched at the end of the day. If only she had another pair of gloves, it might have been a bit easier. She looked at the threadbare, dark blue wool gloves that were issued to the street sweepers two years ago. The fingers had long since worn out and the palms were stuffed with old newspapers. Her long thin fingers were always swollen and in the winter her palms bled, causing the paper stuffed inside to stick to them. No matter, she shrugged, she would cope. There was little likelihood that she would ever play the piano again anyway.

Natasha smiled slightly at the persistent memory of smoothing a blue satin sash as she settled lightly on the very edge of a piano bench. Inside the heavy work boots, her toes moved slightly, instinctively feeling for the pedals of the grand piano. The flutters in her stomach began as if she were to begin an important performance. It all seemed so long ago and far away to have been real. She had been dreaming lately of applause and pieces of familiar-sounding movements. Classical bits and pieces that she could no longer identify. If anyone were to remind her of the fame she once tasted, she would have simply shrugged and said, "What does it matter anymore? I am a street sweeper now."

For almost ten years, she had pulled, dragged and pushed the heavy drum. She learned to keep the wheels greased and the outside of it clean. She even hung a wire across the handles and attached to it some artificial flowers, taken from an old dress she owned. Cleaning the streets of Khursk was far from what she imagined only a few years ago; but it was her livelihood now and she did the best job possible. Some days were especially hard, but there were many that were pleasant. With a smile turning up the corners of her thin, delicate mouth, Natasha concentrated on the task at hand, no matter how much clutter was in the streets. In an organized, determined manner, she attacked each piece of paper lying there with a sense of purpose. This was her assigned duty and she was grateful for the sense of accomplishment it gave her. At only fifty-five years of age, Natasha's small body ached badly at night and her legs would have muscle spasms from the heavy drum when it was full.

The first few months were demanding. Although she quickly learned to maneuver the dented drum up and down the curbstones, her back often ached from bending to pick up cast-off wrappers and cigarettes from the street. People were much messier than she ever imagined. Painful blisters broke open on her feet, which swelled to twice their normal size. Back then, three years ago, Natasha never noticed the pain in her body. The pain in her heart overshadowed it.

Winters were the hardest time for her, but they were offset by the warmth of spring, bringing with it the songs of birds and the smell of flowers. "With every hardship comes a gift," was the old saying, and now it was early summer and Natasha sang along with the birds as she did her job. She was by nature a gregarious woman, speaking easily with people along her route, sometimes scolding someone if she caught them dropping litter. As a result, her sector was the cleanest quadrant in Khursk's busy commercial area.

There had been happy moments in her life, but they all seemed part of the shadows now. The years had gone by quickly, but in many ways, time had stood still for her. The drum had to be returned to the storage yard no later than six o'clock and when Natasha glanced at the clock mounted on the bank, she realized her day's work was almost over. She had not finished her sector and knew that she would probably not receive her full salary. That is, whenever her salary resumed.

The pay had once been substantial, almost enough for a decent life. At least she had been able to buy vegetables and bread and meat on occasion. There was a time when being a sanitation worker was a coveted position and Natasha was considered fortunate by many. Lately, however, even bread was often beyond her means. She hoped the moratorium on government wages would soon be over and those like her would again receive their monthly salaries. The last four months had been long and hard without any money at all for her arduous hours of street sweeping. The allowance given to her each month by her solicitor was barely enough to keep food on the table, and she wondered how others without an extra sum coming in each month were surviving. There were rumors each month that the wages would be released, but each month, it was the same. The window of the paymaster would be closed tightly, with the metal shutters locked and no one around to listen to the complaints.

Last month, only a few of the workers had assembled to protest unlike the early months of the moratorium, but the numbness of apathy had finally taken its toll. After all, little could be done about it. Natasha and her fellow workers had to survive by sheer force of will and ingenuity during these troubled times and most continued on with their duties. Quitting the job would have been futile—there were no other jobs available. At least they would still have a position if the moratorium was ever lifted.

Throughout the former Soviet Union, jobs were becoming scarce. The promised economic reforms were slow in showing results. Hopes for the future of the new republics were high, but showing signs of unrest lately. Demonstrations were becoming more common as the weeks turned into months and patience wore thin. Strikes by various labor groups had halted trains, causing massive disruptions everywhere. Miners and even medical workers had protested in the streets. The scarcity of everyday items was not the problem it had been in the past. Goods from all over the world were in plentiful supply, but prices for them were out of reach for most working people. The economic collapse of the currency touched everyone, but particularly the older citizens.

Suddenly, with an earsplitting screech of brakes, a long black car swerved wildly as Natasha began to cross Sovjetskaja Street. Slamming first into the trash drum and then careening wildly up the curb, the car came to rest against the side of a building. The driver was slumped over the steering wheel. Drunk from an afternoon of drowning his sorrows with cheap vodka, young Sasha Yosenovich had broken his neck and died instantly. When the police arrived, moments later, they made no attempt to revive the young man. Accidents caused by drinking were not unusual. Drunkenness was pervasive in Russian society and the results were often devastating. Wages were often paid in cases of vodka instead of rubles these days. On every street corner, as well as in the underground metro, wives were selling vodka. They bartered the bottles for a few eggs or a bit of bread for their families.

As they stood surveying the crash site, a young officer told the others to be quiet. "I think I hear something!" He listened carefully and moved toward the source of the sound. It seemed to be coming from under a pile of garbage and twisted metal. Stepping carefully, he lifted the heavy drum and discovered the helpless form of Natasha Vassilyeva. Nearly unconscious, but softly moaning, she was placed in the back of the police car and taken to the huge brick building of the Khursk Regional Health Clinic.

Natasha awakened hours later to the sound of voices and a severe headache.

"It is amazing that this old woman was not injured more severely," Ludmilla Morokevna said softly.

"Yes, other than some deep bruises and the cut on her leg, she should recover quickly," said Head Trauma Nurse, Ekaterina Pilovna.

The two nurses hurried to the next bed in the ward. The Charity Wing of the drafty old building was filled to capacity this week. No doubt this was due to the last wave of influenza that took advantage of the most vulnerable, the children and the elderly. The pensioners seemed to arrive in waves. Many of them had been diagnosed with either malnutrition or pneumonia. Most had very little immunity to simple colds and severe bronchial infections became fatal because of it. Natasha, realizing where she was, was frightened to find herself in this place.

A hospital was normally the last place anyone wanted to be, but it was worse these days. The lack of medical supplies and lack of funds for staffing made conditions life threatening for anyone seriously injured. The problems were so numerous that medical care seemed archaic. Power outages during surgery, lack of sterilization equipment, no method of keeping extra blood on hand for transfusions, no laundry facilities for clean linens, not enough food—the list grew longer each day. Fortunate patients had relatives bring in bedding, cooked nutritious food, and soap to wash with. The unfortunate ones, without outside help, simply hoped they survived long enough to leave. It was little wonder that Natasha was frightened when she realized she was in the hospital ward. Luckily, her condition was not serious.

The two nurses, Ekaterina and Ludmilla, continued their rounds and would not likely see her again. Natasha would be released with a small dressing on her leg without an x-ray for a possible broken bone—there was no film for the x-ray machine. It would not have made much difference, the treatment for a broken bone was simply a sling or a crude wooden splint wrapped with a torn-up sheet. Medication for the cut on her leg was an ointment of boric acid and petroleum jelly. She would be given a small packet of it and sent on her way. There would be no battery of tests and no further inquiry into her condition. Although Natasha had been placed in a ward with fifty other patients, there was no such thing as a privacy curtain. Modesty was an unknown word and people wandered about, some confused and disoriented; and fights broke out occasionally as people forgot which bed they were supposed to be in.

Both Ludmilla and Ekaterina had almost grown past the point of concern for their patients. This attitude developed out of necessity. Powerless to change the conditions for their patients, they had to put aside the usual empathy associated with their profession. This shield of armor was often mistaken for insensitivity, which was far from reality. Along with antiquated nursing methods, medical personnel faced many serious, life-threatening diseases that had been all but eradicated in industrialized countries. Typhoid outbreaks were even being seen again in some of the larger cities where the water and sewer systems dated back to the Tsar's rule. Morale sank lower each day, leaving only the most dedicated, as well as those with nowhere else to find work, to staff the last few state-run clinics and hospitals that remained open. Privatization had brought in foreign investments to other institutions, but the needs for this old building and its overcrowded Charity Ward had not attracted investment money. It had become a dumping ground for the voiceless.

As so many others in the medical profession, Ludmilla, the assistant to the Head Nurse, held two jobs and worked seven days a week. She was always tired and often ill, forcing her mind and body to function through the exhaustion. Fortunately, Ludmilla had no family to support, unlike her co-worker Ekaterina, with two small boys at home and an aging mother. Lately, Ekaterina had been talking about leaving her job to find work in a textile factory. The hours would be long and the work hard, but at least she would be paid regularly. Ludmilla, responsible only to herself, understood. Even with her small extra job, she had difficulty. If not for sharing a cramped apartment with four other single women, she would have had to leave also. The low pay and long hours had reluctantly caused many medical professionals to find other jobs. If Ekaterina were to leave, it would mean Ludmilla would have to assume her duties. How she would manage the additional paperwork and meetings worried her constantly and she prayed that Ekaterina would stay.

Ludmilla's natural calling was nursing and she desperately wanted to stay in the field. Even as a child, she could be found wrapping bandages around her dolls, giving them each a spoonful of water "medicine." There was no doubt in anyone's mind as she grew up that she would become a nurse.

Evening came and Ludmilla was hurrying to finish her duties when she heard soft crying from the bed in the corner. "That is the woman struck by the drunkard," she recalled. "She should be sleeping with the sedative I gave her." Ludmilla approached the bed and quietly said, "Is there anything I can do for you?"

Natasha opened her eyes and looked deeply into the clear blue eyes of the young nurse leaning over her. In those eyes, she saw understanding and compassion and sensed that this very tired girl genuinely cared about others. The feeling was not born out of duty; instead she felt a personal warmth uncommon among strangers. Instinctively, Natasha reached out her hand as with a plea for help and Ludmilla took it and held it gently.

Natasha began rambling her thoughts to the blonde nurse with the clear blue eyes. She was talking in half-sentences about a glamorous life, a fantasy life, a fulfilling life. She spoke of audiences and applause and mentioned many names of musical composers. "Chopin, Bach, Mozart, I know them well," she murmured. The sedative she had been given to quiet her through the night caused her to confuse times and events; but Ludmilla listened, hoping her patient would drift off to sleep again. She nodded from time to time while holding the weathered and callused hand. Ludmilla thought of her second job and realized she would be very late again. "Thank God my Uncle is so forgiving and will understand that my nursing duties take precedence over anything else. He will grumble and complain, but I will work extra time for him as usual to make up the work," she thought.

As Natasha began to speak, Ludmilla recognized an educated woman. At first, thinking the woman was delusional, Ludmilla sought only to comfort her; however as Natasha's words became more coherent, she began to understand the story she was telling was true.

Natasha began her disjointed story with the most important element—her love for Viktor, her husband. Listening intently as Natasha's words became slower and choked with emotion, the nurse leaned closer to hear her barely audible whispers. Ludmilla realized the story was causing her more pain than her injuries. The young nurse encouraged her to continue, instinct telling her it would be healing for her to let it come out. In the dream-state of the sedative, Natasha began to release the grief she had been holding inside for so long. The color from her face was gone as she recalled the most difficult events of her life.

For two decades Natasha and Viktor had shared their lives happily, until the day he collapsed and his warm and loving heartbeat was silenced forever. He was alone at the time, in a hotel room in St. Petersburg when it happened. Natasha had been out shopping for shoes and the guilt of not being with him continued to haunt her. Ludmilla stroked Natasha's curly brown hair and softly urged her to continue. The two women's paths had crossed and neither understood the profound impact this would have on the future. Tears began to roll silently down Natasha's still beautiful face, but she continued, "If only I had not wanted another pair of red shoes, perhaps I could have done something to keep him with me." Her voice quivered as she struggled through the rest of the story with great difficulty. She had returned to the hotel and was stopped by the concierge in the lobby. He told her that Viktor had been taken to the hospital. The look in his eyes told her he was holding something back. Immediately, Natasha asked about his condition and the man looked away and sadly shook his head, "I am afraid, Madame Vassilyeva, that it was not in time to save his life. I am so sorry to be the one to tell you this."

In a panic, she took a taxi to the hospital, only to be told that he had been transported to the mortuary. She arrived at the mortuary, sobbing uncontrollably and was told that he was in the preparation room and she could not see him. After painfully making arrangements to send him home to Moscow, she took the taxi back to the hotel. When she arrived at the hotel in a haze of disbelief, she was handed a message. It was from an admirer with a request for tickets for the performance that evening. Suddenly Natasha realized she was supposed to perform in only a few hours. Grief stricken, but obligated by her contract and her sense of duty, she forced herself to dress, with Viktor's belongings all over the hotel room. Still in shocked disbelief, she took a taxi to the concert hall, expecting to see Viktor there when she arrived.

Badly shaken, she arrived within minutes of the orchestra being seated. Visibly upset, she told the concert master that she had been told Viktor was dead, but they were wrong and he would be there very soon—she was sure of it.

Seeing her distress, Master Oleg Popovitch, renowned symphony conductor, patted her shoulder. Kindly, he said, "Viktor would have wanted you to perform your very best tonight. Play only for him and he will hear you when he arrives."

Natasha did perform, glancing toward the wings from time to time, but playing the best she could. First, a Polonaise in F-sharp Minor, Opus 44, by Chopin. This was a technically difficult piece, but one that showed her mastery of the piano with its intricate melody. Next was a robust performance of Brahms' Piano Concerto No. 2. Still glancing over toward the wings, Natasha began to think, "Where is Viktor? He is not there and nothing *ever* kept him away from a performance. He *knows* I need him when I am out here alone on the stage. Where could he *be*? Something dreadful must have happened or he would be here."

Her thoughts raced wildly through the standing ovation and the curtain calls. Painfully, she managed to smile as she accepted the bouquets of flowers from the little girls who came on stage with the huge bows in their hair. "Viktor would be so proud of this concert. But, *where, where* is he?" she frantically said to herself. The curtain came down and blackness overtook her as she remembered the concierge in the hotel lobby. After taking her final bow, Natasha walked unsteadily off the stage and once out of sight of the audience, she collapsed.

This had all happened over ten years ago and the brilliant pianist had not performed publicly since then. Natasha told the nurse how handsome and strong Viktor was, and then drifted off to sleep, leaving Ludmilla with tears glistening in her eyes.

She released her hold on her patient's hand and left the room, but only to call her Uncle Ivan and explain. He rarely inquired about her work, but since she seemed more anxious than normal, he began to ask questions about this particular patient and why she was more upset than usual. Ludmilla attempted to outline the basic facts, without mentioning the patient's name, but Ivan said, "I think this woman is Vassilyeva, is it not? She disappeared from sight after her husband's sudden death. I heard her play in Moscow many times. Such a terrible waste to give up a talent such as hers. Everyone wondered what became of her. If this woman is a beauty, then surely it must be her."

"Yes, Uncle, it is the same woman, but she is dressed in the uniform of a street sweeper and her beauty has suffered quite a bit."

"Well, child," said Ivan to his favorite niece. "It sounds to me that the medicine for her would be a dose of music. You take all the time you need from the bookkeeping work—I will pay you anyway."

When Ludmilla returned to Natasha's bedside, she found her awake again and willing to continue her story.

Viktor Ivanovitch Vassilyeva had been by Natasha's side for over twenty years. He was a friend first, a trusted loyal friend, long before he became her husband.

They met at an informal gathering of student musicians from the Moscow Conservatory where they were all completing their studies. That beautiful spring day had turned into a celebration of sorts. The winner of the coveted award for Piano Excellence in Interpretation had just been announced and Natasha won for the second time. This was a difficult competition, placing her against the most gifted young pianists from all corners of the Soviet Union. The announcement came at the end of classes for the day and her friends insisted on a celebration. "You can be sure of a seat in the touring company now, Natasha!" they kept telling her. The touring company position meant that she would travel, not only in her country, but sometimes to foreign capitals. Closely watched of course by secret police *bodyguards*—she might even get to go to America!

Ludmilla smiled when she saw the older woman's eyes light up as she rambled on. Long into the night, Natasha continued to tell her story. It was as if the words and memories had been unleashed and she couldn't stop the flow of thoughts that had been bottled up in her mind for so long. The nurse understood this and gave her time to unburden herself. Sometimes in whispers, sometimes in the lilting singsong voice of a child, Natasha began to see with clarity for the first time since losing Viktor. As if a fog had lifted, the comforting presence of the blue-eyed nurse gave her the strength needed to explain her situation. She told Ludmilla of her travels to Helsinki, Paris, Bern, and other foreign capitals of the world. She told her of lost luggage and beautiful cathedrals and museums.

Ludmilla, who had never been outside of Khursk, was enthralled by this patient with the callused hands and the clothes of a street sweeper. She noticed that Natasha focused on happy moments, leaving out the painful portions that she could not yet revisit. As Ludmilla watched her face and listened intently, Natasha grew silent and began to cry softly. She drifted off to sleep again, this time the deep breathing confirming a sound rest. Her dreams, again an escape to a safe place, took her to Sergei's home many years ago. As sleep took her away from today and placed her in yesterday, the young nurse softly left her side, knowing there would be another time when she would hear the rest of the story of this once-beautiful and famous woman.

In Natasha's dreams, the apartment of Sergei Rostovich was filled with laughter. Viktor was holding the center of attention with his humorous impressions. His mimicry of the professors at the Conservatory entertained his friends quite often. Viktor could scold like Professor Rinkov, he could lisp in the falsetto of Professor Ulich and his antics made the beautiful Natasha, sitting on the couch, laugh so hard that tears rolled down her cheeks. Viktor's playful nature and keen wit made him a popular student, in spite of his rather weak musical talent. He played the cello, not well, but as he would always say, "with great pleasure." His beaming smile showed perfectly straight white teeth and his thick black hair appeared to always need a haircut. It wasn't his looks or his humor, but his attention to the needs of others that had eventually won Natasha's heart. Without a natural gift for music, Viktor practiced diligently for hours with his cello. He showed an amazing knowledge of composition and love of classical music that drew them closer each day. As Natasha's skills improved, she drew from Viktor's appreciation of the mind of the masters. From him, she learned the foundation beneath the music she played.

She learned that Frederick Chopin had been buried with an urn of Polish soil that he had carried with him everywhere he went until his death from tuberculosis. The fragile nature of Chopin's music reflected a gentle heart and the fragility of life that filled her spirit as she played. Quite often, just for him, Natasha played Viktor's favorite piece, Chopin's difficult Barcarolle F-sharp Major, Opus 60. He knew when she played that particular piece that it was for his benefit and his beaming smile lit up the room. Their eyes would connect and she felt her spine tingle as if it were a vibrating violin string. Spending many hours together, discussing theory and timing. Viktor's perceptive nature of the masters began to permeate her performances—the feeling flowing from her heart to her fingers. Recognition of her talent increased. Natasha began first to win local competitions and as her fame grew, so did her love for Viktor. They were married in a small civil ceremony, without friends and family, in between performances. Viktor always felt badly about the simple ceremony, but until they left student status, their finances were very weak. He slowly began to manage her career and together they traveled throughout the Empire and abroad. Their love and respect for one another continued to grow and life slowly became one of pleasure and privilege.

With Viktor's death, Natasha's entire world collapsed. She knew nothing of their finances and was shocked to find there was so little put aside for emergencies. The solicitor released small amounts of money to her each month, but with increased prices, it was barely enough to exist on. Natasha was now a widow, and as such, was gradually left out of social engagements. Her mental and physical condition after the funeral caused cancellation of numerous performances and she lost the contacts needed for promotion and agents needed to arrange private tours. As usual in the theatrical world, fame is indeed fleeting and the clamor for new talent always changes rapidly. Natasha withdrew psychologically and formed a shell around herself. After Viktor's death, she was no longer a spirited personality; for without his protective arm around her, she felt half a person.

Grief had taken a physical toll on her body as well. She became gaunt, with cheekbones like saw blades and arms as thin as nails. Without Viktor to remind her to eat, Natasha spent hours mindlessly playing simple mazurkas and nocturnes over and over again, staring blankly into space. With the slightest sound, she would jump off the piano bench and run to the door, hoping it was Viktor's key in the lock. The reality of Viktor never coming through the door again wearing his wide, dazzling smile, would strike with such force at times that Natasha would simply crumble to the floor in anguish. Waves of sorrow would overcome her and she would sleep to escape the thoughts that invaded her sanity. In a heap, under the piano, she would stare at the legs of the ornate piano bench for hours.

Eventually, Natasha only left the apartment to go to the market at the end of the street, often believing she had to meet Viktor somewhere. People who knew her would give her food and direct her to her home. Three years before, Sergei, their mutual friend from the Conservatory, saw her one day on the street, he almost did not recognize her. Was this the beautiful, fastidious Natasha, the gifted pianist, who could bring an audience to their feet? Was this disheveled, dirty wisp of a woman the same girl who once stood proudly accepting bouquets with grace and humility? Sergei was both shocked and saddened by her appearance. Standing before him, with head down and looking rather lost, this woman was a ghost of whom he remembered. Sergei Rostovich took her by the arm and escorted her to her home. Once inside, Sergei was dumbfounded by what he saw in the beautifully appointed apartment. Filth covered the place. Days-old food had been left lying about; dishes and the smell of decay permeated everything. Once inside the familiar surroundings, Natasha immediately went over and sat on the edge of the piano bench. There with her slumping shoulders, oblivious to Sergei and everything else, she began to play.

Sergei listened and thought he heard Tchaikovsky's Concerto No.1 in B-flat Major, at least a semblance of it. It somehow seemed to fit that Tchaikovsky's sad life would inspire her to play his music. "The elementals were still there," thought Sergei. He listened more and analyzed, "The structure and the harmony are evident, but the rhythm was mechanical and does not display the sensitive touch that I know she is capable of performing." This became more pronounced as the artist moved into a nocturne by Chopin. It sounded as brusque as Rachmaninov! This was *not* the Natasha that Sergei remembered, and he shook his head sadly and choked back tears.

He left her there, to her grief-inspired performance, and went directly home to talk to his wife, Svetlana. Listening carefully to her husband's anguish at the decline of their friend over these months after Viktor's death, Svetlana suggested that they try to find something else to fill the void in Natasha's life. "Perhaps a job would help, something to take her away from her surrounding?" she offered. They both thought for a moment and Svetlana said, "Nature is such a miracle worker and it's spring now, such a beautiful time of year. I have an idea! Let me make some phone calls and try to bring her back before she leaves for good."

Svetlana's calls included one to her cousin, Igor. As the head of the Health and Sanitation Labor Union, Igor had the right connections. After listening to Svetlana's concerns, he agreed to help. The next day, he called back and told Svetlana that Natasha was approved, by his recommendation, to be assigned to the Khursk commercial area near her apartment, as a street sweeper. Sergei and Svetlana went to Natasha's filthy apartment the next day and gently explained that it was for her own good that they arranged this and that it would be just like a performance. She had to report at an appointed time and simply do as she was told.

Sergei told her, "The salary is good and you will meet people who work in many different businesses. You will be outside in the fresh air and sunshine, listening to the church bells and the birds and seeing the children all day."

"Plus," continued Svetlana, "you need this money right now, dear friend, or how will you live if you can't pay for the apartment?"

Finally Natasha agreed, saying with a shrug, "What does it matter anyway? I will do whatever you say." There was no reluctance in her voice, only resignation.

The following morning, Natasha Vassilyeva began her first day as a sweeper for the Khursk Sanitation District. Svetlana had spent the night with her and after she bathed and put Natasha to bed, she cleaned up the apartment a bit. In the morning, she drove her to the District offices where they gave her a uniform and a large apron-like covering for it. She was handed a broom and when Svetlana left, her friend was diligently looking for papers and trash. She was responsible for an area from Sovjetskaya Street on the north side to Leningradskaya on the south. The eastern boundary was the river and the western boundary, a park. The entire area was approximately one-half mile square and relatively busy with office buildings and financial businesses. At first, Natasha swept in one spot for an hour before moving on to the next, but she learned quickly when shopkeepers or policemen scolded her and she was forced to move along.

In a few days, she became compulsive in her attempts to keep her area clean. Each morning, she inspected available brooms from a pile at the drum storage area-taking her time to find the best one. After a while, not finding ones to her liking, she made her own. Fine brooms of willow branches they were, with short handles for her short arms. Vigorously, she worked her broom across the cobblestone streets. Wearing the apron that was standard issue for all street sweepers, she seemed proud of her "uniform." Most of the sweepers left their aprons overnight at the pickup area, but Natasha took hers home and washed it on her days off, laying it in the sun on the windowsill to bleach it as white as possible. She did the same with the head-scarf and it was always clean. She tied bright-colored ribbons to her apron, which made her instantly recognizable to the shopkeepers who began to wave to her when she passed by. They knew it was good for business if the front of their shops were kept clean and she would often receive fruit or vegetables for her efforts. Without leaving even a tiny scrap of paper behind, she filled her trash drum to overflowing each night. After months of scrutinizing every inch of her area, Natasha began to relax and enjoy what she had accomplished. As she pushed her broom, she was often heard humming and the pushing began to have a rhythmic movement as well.

Natasha also began to pay more attention to her appearance and often tied her long hair back with ribbons. When she returned home in the evening, she cleaned up the apartment a bit at a time, until it was again a showplace for her beautiful belongings. She dusted all the delicate souvenirs collected from the concert tours and rearranged the expensive vases that Viktor always bought for the bouquets she received from her admirers after a concert. The one thing that Natasha could not bring herself to wax and dust was the grand piano in the corner. To avoid seeing the instrument, she had covered it with a large cloth. Not large enough to hide it completely, the legs of the ornate piano bench still showed beneath it.

The bench had been a gift from Viktor on their tenth wedding anniversary. He secretly purchased it from an antique shop in France and had to enlist the aid of the constant KGB escorts who accompanied them on all their travels outside the country. It was difficult to arrange, but he succeeded in convincing them that this was something his wife would need to enhance her performances. In his playful way, he persuaded the agents to help him substitute her usual plain bench for the new one without telling her. When she walked across the stage to take her seat at the instrument, he watched her wide-eyed look of surprise as he stood in his usual position in the wings with his beaming smile. She lightly sat on the edge of the bench and felt his love for her flowing like warm syrup through her entire body from the new bench.

For the next twenty years, the bench traveled with them. Protected with rugs, it became a symbol of their love, both of music and of each other. Natasha had lovingly traced the designs with her fingertips hundreds of times over the years. Using only the most expensive oils to polish its delicate inlays, the bench had never as much as squeaked or even loosened its doweled joints.

Since Viktor's death, however, the ornately carved legs of the mahogany bench were almost hidden beneath a layer of grime and dust. The seat top would not even close completely. Filled with sheet music that had not been played for years, the lid gaped open, its contents peeking out from one side as if beckoning to her. Natasha could hardly bear to look at it and so it sat, half hidden, a constant reminder of what *used* to be.

The hospital was supposed to release Natasha the next morning; however Ludmilla conveniently "forgot" to fill out the forms, giving them one more day to visit together. Ludmilla smiled or waved each time she passed her patient's bed and the old woman smiled back at her. Natasha had thoughts of inviting the pleasant young nurse with the striking blue eyes to visit her while she convalesced. She missed having guests, although Sergei and Svetlana stopped by from time to time. It was obvious that she would not be returning to her work with her broom for quite some time. The cut on her leg was very serious and the wound had to kept scrupulously clean, lest it become infected. In addition, in her condition it took a long time for injuries to heal. She also had some deep purple bruises on her back.

Natasha's final words before leaving the Charity Ward were simply said, "I was once very happy, but now I cannot remember what happiness feels like most of the time. You were so kind to listen to the ramblings of an old woman and I would be pleased if you would come to see me when you have a little time."

Ludmilla, touched by her patient's lonely fragility and sincerity, agreed. They kissed, embraced and parted company.

It was two days before Ludmilla could find a bit of free time to spare. During those two days, Natasha occupied her thoughts. She had found out only a small part of Natasha's life and wanted to get to know her better. She telephoned and made arrangements to look in on her and check the progress of the wound. Knowing very little about the world of concerts and classical music, the young nurse had no way of comprehending the world she was about to enter.

Ludmilla arrived at Natasha's apartment late in the afternoon. Natasha had placed the little she had to eat on her beautiful table, set with silver and her best china. The setting was elegant and the two women sat and talked easily, at time laughing as they poked fun at the current politicians and their promises. It was common for Russians to use humor when discussing difficulties in their country in the privacy of their homes. The criticisms had a stinging wit and more than an element of truth behind them. As Ludmilla relaxed, she gazed around the room and could not help noticing the cloth-draped distinct shape of a piano in the corner. Natasha noticed Ludmilla's eyes shift to the corner and abruptly began another subject. Ludmilla caught the nuance and decided quickly not to mention the piano at all. Natasha relaxed, realizing the topic would not be brought up. Soon after, Ludmilla had to leave and after closing the door, Natasha sank into a soft chair and began to drift off into restless sleep.

It would be a week before Ludmilla returned to visit her friend. The Head Nurse, Ekaterina, had been ill and could not come to work, leaving Ludmilla to work extra hours without pay to keep up with patient care and the mounting paperwork. She was exhausted when she knocked on the apartment door. The pretty nurse was pleased at the change in her friend's appearance and attitude. The respite from the toil of sanitation labor had done the old woman well and it showed. There was a sparkle in her eyes and she greeted Ludmilla with a warm hug and a big smile. Pulling out the high-backed dining chairs, they sat down to talk. The silver tea service was set out and the samovar bubbled. Ludmilla noticed that the tea was barely colored water and knew the old woman was using the very last of what she had to order. There were eight crackers on a silver serving tray and Ludmilla scolded herself for not bringing a small gift of food with her. She vowed not to forget the next time, ate one cracker and claimed she was full. From her vantage point, Ludmilla could see the piano in the corner. She wanted so much to hear Natasha play, but did not know how to approach the subject.

After checking the wound, which was healing nicely with no signs of infection, the young nurse began to tell her of recent events at the Charity Clinic. Natasha listened intently, always hoping for the politicians' promises to become a reality. Her interest increased when Ludmilla began to tell her of the children in the pediatric ward. "They are the saddest ones of all," Ludmilla said. "Many parents cannot come to see them because they are working all the time. The hospital does not have the funds to buy toys or games for them and so they sit for hours, doing nothing at all. There is no longer staff to visit with them and those of us who are still there simply do not have the time. Many are so sick they just lie there and look at the ceiling. We don't have medicine to treat them and sometimes the children are brought in for help and just left there. No one comes to take them home. I just have to walk away in tears. If investors don't come soon, I doubt the Clinic will be open much longer." Natasha had tears in her eyes as she heard the story. Ludmilla continued, "We have had strong rumors lately of another medical science investor group from France, but like the others, this one will probably never be heard from, like all the others."

The thought of the children had touched Natasha deeply. She had never had children, nor did she ever want them when it was possible. Her career had been too important and time consuming for children and Viktor was in agreement with her. He always told her that as long as they had each other, there was no room for anyone else. Many times she wondered if he said that only because he thought she wanted to hear it. Since Viktor's death, Natasha regretted the decision made so many years before.

With Viktor gone, she was all alone. There were no children and, of course, would be no grandchildren. She often stopped her sweeping to talk to the children who were with their parents on the streets. The little ones in their carriages would smile and coo back at her when she sang to them or made funny sounds. She often wished Viktor could see her being silly as he used to be so long ago. The shy toddlers would hide behind their mother's skirts, peeking out with curiosity. Natasha would play the age-old game of "Peekaboo" with them and they would giggle with delight. Sometimes their mothers would say to them, "Say thank you to Babushka," and that would make Natasha cringe. She was *not* a true "grandmother" and would never be one, so she decided to be a Babushka only when she was sweeping.

Ludmilla continued, "There is one child in particular. His name is Alexei and he is only three years old and very ill. He does not speak a word and the woman from the orphanage that sent him says he has never spoken. No one really knows what kind of illness he has and we don't have the facilities to treat him..."

"Is the child deaf?" Natasha interrupted.

"Oh no," said Ludmilla, "In fact, one thing I noticed is that he seems to like music." Seizing the opening, she continued, trying not to look toward the piano, "When I go near his bed, I sing to him and he smiles at me." Taking a slight breath, she continued, "Do you know any songs for children, Natasha?"

Natasha hestitated for only a moment and then nodded. "I used to play a lullaby by Brahms a long time ago. He was not my favorite, but everyone knows his work, so it was required when I was a student at the Conservatory."

Again, sensing the door begin to open, Ludmilla continued, "I'm afraid I wouldn't know any. I don't have much knowledge of music, but if Brahms is not your favorite composer, then who *is* your favorite one?" Natasha rose and walked to the window. Ludmilla's heart leapt to her throat. Fearing she had gone too far, she wished she had not pressed her friend on this sensitive part of her life.

Gazing out onto the street below, Natasha softly answered, "I appreciate all the masters, child. Each one has his own strengths and weaknesses. A favorite piece of music is as impossible to choose as a favorite hair in one's head, or a favorite finger of a hand." These were the words often spoken by Viktor, and Natasha hearing herself say them, could not help but smile.

"But surely," Ludmilla asked gently, "some are more complicated or difficult? Some are more happy or sad?"

Natasha laughed. "Well, of course, some require constant practice to maintain competence." She continued, embracing the subject, "Tchaikovsky, for example, struggled with his homosexuality. The passions he expressed are reflected in the power of his compositions. There is still mystery concerning his death. Some claim it was cholera, others that it was related to his personal life and had to do with a former lover." Natasha began to talk faster and with animation in her voice. She recounted details of other composers and Ludmilla listened with rapt attention. "Fredric Chopin, for example, wrote complicated melodies and some of them I worked on for years before I could play them."

Ludmilla seized the opportunity. "The door is open wide enough now," she thought. As Natasha was talking, Ludmilla had inched her way toward the drape-covered piano. Lifting a corner of the white fabric, she gently said, "Would you show me what you mean, Natasha?"

The old woman hesitated briefly and sighed. "Dear child, I have not touched this piano in many years." Looking down at her hands, she continued softly, "I don't even know if I remember anymore; but since you don't know him, let me introduce you to a bit of Chopin's work."

Ludmilla smiled as she uncovered the piano and its bench. Natasha removed a folded piece of sheet music from the piano bench and swallowed hard before settling her small body down on the edge. Biting her lower lip, Ludmilla held her breath, not daring to speak for fear of saying the wrong thing and breaking the moment. Natasha extended her fingers above the keys, but not touching them. She stretched her legs and gauged the distance to the pedals. Ludmilla watched as she seemed to be collecting her thoughts. The silence in the room was almost unbearable. Then, it happened.

The room became filled with waves of music. Timidly at first, then with increased confidence and finally, with a surety born of innate talent and years of practice, the crescendos of Fredric Chopin's music filled the room. Ludmilla felt tears burn her eyes as her friend revealed her skill. It was as if Natasha had been transported to another place and time. Her eyes closed and her body swayed with the emotions of the music. Flawlessly, her hands traversed the keyboard, gently retreating and then passionately assaulting, bringing forth the intensity and the tenderness of the piece. As Natasha played, she felt her soul being released from its exile of the past. She proceeded through a lively mazurka to a lilting polonaise and then to a pleading nocturne. The intricate melodies seemed to inhale and exhale along with Natasha as the instrument breathed life into her. They became one force, and the room reverberated with energy. With a final series of light touches, sensing the importance of what she had just done, the artist in her knew it was time to stop.

Silence again filled the room, deafening silence when the echoes of the last note faded. Ludmilla was speechless with wonder and overcome with emotion. *Never* in her life had she heard such beauty from a piece of wood and a human being blended in such a mystical union.

Natasha shook her head, as if to clear her mind. She sighed and looked up at the young woman. Noticing tears still wet on her cheeks,

Natasha smiled. "You *feel* the music, my child, that is good. Music is *meant* to reach into the soul, but I am afraid I did not do it justice. I have been out of practice for a long time, maybe too long."

Ludmilla was astonished. "No, no, you were wonderful! It was beautiful, so very, very beautiful. I felt like dancing and like flying and my heart was ready to burst." She sputtered, unable to describe the impact of the music in mere words. The two women smiled at each other, each sharing the other's joy of the moment.

Natasha was suddenly tired and slightly slumped on the bench. Ludmilla knew it was time to leave and allow her friend to absorb what had just transpired. She helped Natasha to cover the piano again and made a silent promise to herself that somehow she would influence Natasha to play again. "It would be such a tragic loss if she turned to her broom again and shut her gifts off from others," she thought. Ludmilla knew she would have to act quickly. Natasha would be called to return to sweeping soon. She could not afford to stay at home. Ludmilla would have to come up with a plan.

The next morning, Natasha looked at the drape-covered piano for very long time. Twice she walked towards it, only to retreat to the dining room table. She rose the third time and picked up an edge of the drape. "Hello old friend," she said. She made a cup of tea and sat staring at the instrument from the table with remorse. Finally, with firm and deliberate steps, she walked over to it and pulled the drape off, leaving it in a heap on the floor. Lifting the keyboard cover, she noticed the keys had yellowed a tiny bit and pressing down on some of them realized it was slightly out of tune. She had neglected this part of herself for so long and shook her head sadly. Unfortunately, it would take more money than she had now to get it back into playing condition. The thought suddenly occurred to her that perhaps she could ask her solicitor for an advance! With renewed determination, she resolved to do just that. "I did not realize what I had abandoned until last night," she muttered. She recalled seeing Ludmilla's face and felt her absorb the music, something inside had awakened and she felt herself come alive again. "To see the music reach her in such a way is reason enough for me to play for her again," she thought.

Natasha phoned the solicitor, a compassionate man, originally from Poland. It had been three years since Natasha had spoken to him and she was surprised that he recognized her name so quickly. When Viktor was alive, Stanislaw Wilenski represented them for contracts on many occasions, but Natasha had little interest in contracts and business and avoided such matters entirely. Wilenski sounded pleased to hear her voice and she wondered why he seemed to chuckle slightly throughout their conversation.

Stanislaw was delighted that Natasha wanted to repair the damage that time and lack of use had caused. He recalled how he would often hear her practicing in the background when he was on the telephone with her late husband. Viktor had given him tickets more than once and he admired her tremendously and had been hoping she would call someday. His firm represented Viktor's will and handled the monthly stipend she was receiving as well. There was a condition associated with the stipend, but unless she was performing, it was not to be revealed to her. Stanislaw was a man of honor and, although he was aware she was no longer on the concert tour schedule, he could not interfere with the dictates of the will. His delight at hearing from her now as she explained the need for tuning her fine piano was linked to his knowledge of Viktor's wishes. He readily agreed to the sum she requested and hung up the phone with a smile.

Natasha received the additional money and promptly called the best piano tuner in Khursk. When the wizened old gentleman heard the name Natasha Vassilyeva, he was stunned. It was well known in the tight circle of accomplished musicians that the beautiful woman pianist with so much distinction had given up her gift following the death of her husband and manager. Anatoli Ruvenko was honored to be called upon to repair the instrument of such a talented artist. He knew she would own one of the finest pianos built and that it would challenge his skills. This was far from being called to a dingy apartment to tune a poor quality instrument for a child who pounded the keys with sticky fingers. He brushed his teeth and dressed in his finest clothes, eager to see the piano with which he had been chosen to work.

He was a long way from disappointed on entering the Vassilyeva apartment. The instrument was truly that of concert quality. He was not surprised to see that nothing had been placed on its lid, as one would find in the home of an amateur. He often said, "A piano is not a table, to be used for displays of figurines and keepsakes. It is, instead, to be appreciated for its form and design and stand uncluttered in its beauty." It had recently been polished—Anatoli could smell the exotic Brazilian polish—and it now stood waiting for his delicate touch.

Anatoli was surprised at Natasha's knowledge of the complicated mechanism. She pointed out a hammer that was just barely out of alignment before he had even opened his bag of tools. She also had an acute ear and could distinguish the slightest difference in resonance as he turned the screws connected to the wires ever so slightly. The old craftsman was in awe of the beauty of the ebony wood. It felt warm to the touch and as smooth as satin under his gnarled hands. He caressed the open lid as one would caress a newborn baby, with love and tenderness. The bench—ah, the bench—was a work of artistic beauty. Its tiny inlaid pieces of ivory and the carved scrollwork reminded him of a museum piece. Inset in the legs were various shades of wood, curved with a shell design at the bend of its knees. Anatoli frowned, however, as he noticed the amount of sheet music stuffed under the lid, straining the hinges.

"I think you might want to remove some of the music, Madame Vassilyeva," he said, pointing to the bench. "It would be a pity to see the lid break off those fragile hinges."

Natasha agreed and opened the lid, slowly pulling out papers. She was kneeling on the floor and grabbed a handful of the sheets of music altogether. Some of them fell and scattered on the floor near her. Anatoli was busy under the grand piano and heard a loud gasp, followed by crying. Wiggling out from underneath he watched her for a moment as she held some music and continued to cry. "This was Viktor's favorite, Chopin's Barcarolle, I played it often because he loved it so," she sobbed.

Anatoli looked at the heartbroken woman and with the insight of one who dealt with sensitive artists all his life, he casually asked, "Why don't you play it for him *now*, Madame?"

Looking intently at Anatoli, casually watching her, she started to say something, but he stopped her. "I am finished and need you to play something anyway to test the instrument. Why not play his favorite piece? Trust me, he *will* hear it." With a smooth movement, he pulled the bench closer to the keyboard and wiped it with his polishing cloth with a flourish. He bowed and said firmly, "Please Madame Vassilyeva, please play the Chopin."

Natasha bit her lower lip to keep it from quivering and eased her small body onto the edge of the bench. She had not played since that night for Ludmilla, but this was different. She sat with familiarity, her toes testing the distance to the pedals and her back slightly arched. She positioned herself with her wrists relaxed and her elbows at the precise angle to her body.

Flexing her fingers, she began to feel something peculiar and also familiar happening to her body. There was a warmth rising from the bench, a warmth that flowed through her like warm syrup—it reached her heart in the same manner as the love she felt watching Viktor standing in the wings of the stage. Slowly, Natasha began to play. As the notes of the beautiful and intricate composition of the Barcarolle F-sharp Major, Opus 60, filled the room, a transformation took place. Natasha Vassilyeva was playing with her heart. The beauty of the music itself, combined with her skill, brought the finely tuned piano to life under her touch. The majestic crescendos, with notes scrambling to be heard separately then racing to join together, then dancing like raindrops on a still lake, rising again, creating frantic confusion, in an incredible display of passion, then softened by the gentle touch of tender caresses. It ended with the last single note left hanging in the air, refusing to release itself completely.

There was a moment of reverent silence, then applause broke the stillness. When she finished, Natasha was smiling as Anatoli applauded wildly and bowed to her as if she were royalty—a deep bow, from the waist until his head was almost touching his knees.

More applause came from the doorway, where Sergei and Svetlana were crying as they clapped in unison. Stanislaw was there also, yelling, "Brava, brava!" Natasha slowly stood up and bowed to them, then burst into tears as she realized her music was not *hers*, but belonged to everyone who listened to it.

Svetlana went to fix the samovar for the tea they had brought with them, while Stanislaw presented the check to her for the piano tuning, which she simply signed and handed to Anatoli. Ludmilla had been silently standing in the corner. She stopped by, bringing a message, but had not yet had a chance to relay it. Natasha looked around the room at her friends, both old and new, and said, "Thank you, everyone, for leading me back to where I belong. To be able to convey what the Maestros intended. Their passion, their inner struggles, the messages of love and beauty that you feel, I could see it in your smile," she said, nodding towards Ludmilla, "and in your eyes," looking at Anatoli.

No one spoke as the impact of her words settled into the room. At first, they listened, then spontaneously they all began to clap their hands in admiration. Sensing the opportunity and unable to hold her news in for another moment, Ludmilla spoke, "Natasha, do you remember that I told you there were people interested in keeping the Charity Clinic open?

Well, there was a meeting today and I proposed your name, I hope you don't mind."

"*My* name?" questioned Natasha.

"Yes, *your* name, but if you are not interested, I will understand. The meeting was with some doctors from Austria and the entire staff was required to attend. They talked, of course, about changes they were going to make with our sterilization methods and some other things. But the most important thing they talked about was *music therapy!*"

"Music? What do doctors know of music except buying box seats to a concert?" Everyone laughed.

"Many things, that's why I am so excited. They talked about a center they are going to open in a wing of the Clinic. This music therapy is being used with amazing success! They said that studies are showing changes in health when music is played, different changes for different conditions, something to do with rhythm they say."

"Well child, I have always known that music can heal the spirit, but what does that have to do with me?"

"They are offering a grant of millions of rubles to begin the program and were looking for a Director for it. I mentioned your name and they know of you and would love to have you be in the position. I told them about Alexei, do you remember? I told them how he smiles when I sing to him. They talked of children, like Alexei and his condition, which they say is called *autism*. They think he should be the first case in the new department! May I report to them that you will meet with them and then you won't have to go back to street sweeping ever again and you can save your hands for more important things?" Ludmilla glanced toward the piano.

"Well," said Stanislaw, standing up in the middle of the room. "I too have a bit of news for you, Natasha. Viktor's will has a large sum waiting for you, but it was not to be released unless you continued to perform. With this position the young lady is talking about, you would technically be *performing*, so you would not have to worry about finances."

"And," began Sergei, "if you want to take a trip to Austria to learn more about this Music Therapy, I am sure I can get you back on the concert tour circuit, even if only for two or three performances a year. People have missed you, Natasha."

"Not as much as I have missed them," said Natasha with tears in her eyes. "Not as much as I have missed them."

* * *

The field of Music Therapy has taken great strides in recent years. It has proven effective in working with many psychological illnesses and with people of all ages. Whether music is used to relax with, meditate with, dance to, sing with, or simply enjoy, Natasha hopes that music is always a part of your life—and so does little Alexei, who now has a babushka.

Irina

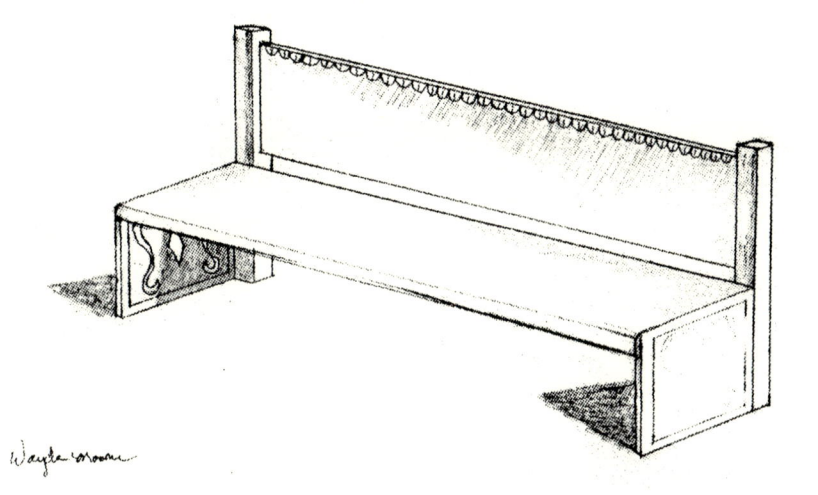

The back of Irina's thick neck was aching again. It was no wonder. She had been in this position far too long for a woman her age. She often lost track of time when she worked in her garden, painstakingly turning the earth, then placing the spent leaves back under the soil. Along with the refuse from the kitchen, the leaves would give the earth back the nourishment it needed for the following year. The crisp autumn smell left little doubt that this was her final harvest of squash and turnips. The rich, black soil was easy to work and its sweet smell confirmed the nutrients in it. The loose earth created a soft carpet under her swollen feet.

She had been in the garden for hours, patiently moving the soil, often with her bare hands. Irina was proud of her small plot of land. Knowing that she was working the same land that her grandparents had cultivated connected her to her history. Irina had no other choice but to spend hours tending her small plot. Although the yield was small, and many of the vegetables oddly deformed, Irina knew too well that a long winter could bring hunger despite her labor. She shivered at the thought of the bitter wind she would soon hear howling outside her log home. Looking up at the log dacha through the hazy curtain of failing sight brought warmth to her seventy-six-year-old heart. It was all that she owned, even though the ground beneath it would never be hers. It would belong to the state, despite the new reforms in her country.

Irina took comfort knowing the dacha itself, with its logs precisely cut and tightly sealed, was safely titled in her name at the Land Ministry Office. Her late husband, Vladimir, made sure of that before his death almost thirty years ago. Irina thought, "Vladimir was meticulous when it came to details." She was proud to have been married to a man such as Vladimir. Such a tall, handsome man he had been before his sickness began. It was easier for Irina to blame his failing health on something other than age. She could not think of Vladimir as simply getting old and wearing out. In her mind there had never been so many years between their ages, and she never considered that he would weaken long before she did. It had been a painful thing for Irina to see his once strong body become frail. When he could no longer bear the weight of two small logs for the fireplace, she once found him weeping outside near the woodpile. That scene had always remained with her. Her dark eyes filling with tears, Irina turned her attention back to her garden.

Irina married Vladimir when she was eighteen years old and the fact that he had been twenty-five years her senior proved to be a blessing. Gentle Vladimir, her towering giant of a husband, was an unusual man. Middle aged before he took a wife, his Cossack heritage gave him a love of nature and a spirit that could not be broken. Often found embroiled in politics, Vladimir could have been called a troublemaker, if one did not know him well. Irina's placid personality and simple, unassuming ways seemed to balance his strong opinions. It was outspoken Vladimir who was the symbol of fairness for those who knew him well. Normally soft-spoken, his voice could become a deafening boom when he discussed the current political leaders, or the lack of what he considered justice. Many times Irina would place her finger to her lips to remind him that others could be listening, but Vladimir would seldom pay attention.

Born in 1886, only five years after the good Tsar Alexander II had been assassinated, Vladimir became Irina's history teacher. From him she had learned of the famine in 1890 that took the lives of thousands of people, including his older brothers and a sister. He had been just a child, but managed to survive, along with his parents, Olga and Boris. Another brother, Anatoly, was born later to Olga who gave her life for his birth. Vladimir and his father Boris raised Anatoly in this village on the banks of the Don River. Irina recalled seeing Boris and his two sons working side by side in the wheat fields together as she was growing up. To her, the Moisevitch family represented the finest in Ukrainian men. Listening to them sing the ancient folk songs of the Cossack campfires, accompanied by the sweet sound of balalaika music, Irina could easily visualize the stories the beautiful music told. Little did she know that Vladimir, the older of the sons, would approach her father for her hand in marriage.

"He is much too old," her friends had told her.

"Yes, but he is the best man in the village," Irina had replied.

Her parents had been more than willing to let their plain, big-boned daughter go to a man whom the entire village admired. They knew that Vladimir Moisevitch, having made a commitment to take a wife, would never allow her to be unprotected. Irina was proud of the fact that Vladimir did not beat her to show his authority in their home. Traditionally, this was accepted behavior, but Vladimir refused, even when he was chided for allowing a woman to have her own way at times. A mutual respect for one another was evident and for Vladimir there was no need to show superiority in his home. Together they had shared a full life. Irina had borne six children, only two of who survived infancy. A small family by the standards of the times, Irina felt fulfilled and complete as long as Vladimir and the children were by her side.

Then after decades of being the center of Irina's life, he died. And now, even though Vladimir had been gone all these years, Irina felt his presence with her still.

He had provided well when he was alive, but many changes had taken place since his death. War, famine, oppression—all of these had touched her. Fortunately, the small farm in Litski was necessary no matter what was going on politically. Armies had to be fed regardless. Even the bureaucrats had to be fed, and so this farm had survived it all.

When the authorities tried to confiscate hidden stores of wheat many years ago, the neighboring farmers locked themselves in the storage barn, along with their wheat. They set fire to themselves rather than give up their stockpiles that would have kept them alive through the winter.

The farmers of Litski, however, gave up their wheat without resistance. Many of them died of starvation, but Vladimir negotiated with the authorities who respected him for his fairness. Almost half of the village had survived those troubled times because of it.

Life was still difficult and Irina had to labor long hours to ensure her survival even now. She relied on her wits and the lessons Vladimir had taught her. Drying and salting, as well as smoking, were skills she had learned well. Every morning she had gone to the river to fish, drying her catch outdoors and placing it in cloth that she saved or for which she traded.

Fall had come to this part of Ukraine. It was harvest time. The potatoes were all dug and buried underground. Cabbages, most weighing up to fifteen pounds apiece, were placed in an earthen pit lined with stones or shredded and placed in salt brine. Carrots, beets, onions and garlic were all being stored in cellars or hung to dry, to be used for the coming winter.

Poor farming practices, and misuse of the land for generations, meant the yields decreased each year. Crop rotation was not implemented and the land had never been allowed to rest. The collective farms had been pushed to the extreme and the results were slowly but surely becoming evident. The crops of the collective farms surrounding the village of Litski were entirely dependent on the weather for moisture since there was no irrigation system. In addition, everyone knew that the land was contaminated by the open nuclear testing. The assurance of the government did not fool the people of the village. Not only did they not trust the claims of Ministry Officials, but they could see for themselves the results of the testing. It took only hours after each thunderous explosion for the "dust" to make their eyes and skin itch unbearably. Numerous miscarriages took place in the villages surrounding the test sites, as well as rumors of babies with horrifying deformities. The people felt little security in their country, but they had no other choices.

Historically, this was the land of the Don Cossack—the land of their ancestors—and it was loved beyond comprehension. To consider leaving their land was unthinkable, and so life would continue as it always had.

Without communication with the rest of the world, information was limited, and often deliberately stifled by the authorities. The residents of Litski lived their lives today as they had for centuries, isolated and unaware of the changes outside of the village.

Change, however, was coming and Irina could sense it. The young people of the village were restless and many had left to seek their fortunes elsewhere. The currency had been devalued many times and most educated people in the country had already emigrated elsewhere. But Irina never ventured more than a few miles beyond Litski, travel being difficult for anyone in this part of the world. The rail lines connecting to the main track had been left untended for many years. Even the famous Trans-Siberian railroad that used to come within thirty-five kilometers of the village ran sporadically now. The "official" explanation was that the neglected switches, with their frequent breakdowns, might strand travelers for hours and even for days on the endless barren stretches across the steppes of Russia. There were virtually hundreds of trains on the tracks throughout the country at the same time, with thousands of tiny villages bypassed and the spurs overlooked for maintenance. The tracks covered at least eight time zones across the old Soviet Empire, so a traffic jam was a nightmare. But no one wanted to take the responsibility for the maintenance across the vast grasslands of the steppes that produced the cereal grains to feed this immense country.

There were few telephones in Litski, and even fewer motor vehicles. An enormous amount of time was spent waiting for the weekly bus, belching its thick oily diesel fuel. The rusty, creaking bus transferred its riders to the train station in Lulursk, the closest city, but a five-hour bus trip away. It was easy to understand why villages remained unchanged for decades, with rail travel necessary to cover the huge expanse.

Despite these difficulties, the people were moving ahead while dragging their government behind them; but progress was hard and old ideas and habits persisted.

Patiently placing some small turnips in her apron, Irina felt the sun warm on her back. "Yes," she thought, "I should have enough food again this winter." Each small harvest from her tiny garden meant survival for another year. She knew it was time to stop when the sun cast its orange-yellow glow over the surrounding hills. Irina, with her feet now painfully swollen, slowly made her way up the hill toward the largest house in the village.

At one time, this was the home of Boris Ivanov, the owner of the entire estate where Irina's Cossack family, only three generations ago, had settled. Her grandfather, Igor, had been registered and as such was not expected to work the fields like a peasant. After all, freedom was the birthright of all Cossacks.

Under Tsar Nicholas, Vladimir had taught her, the serfs had been set free. Many of their descendants now lived in Litski and worked in the immense wheat fields as their great-grandparents before them. Although not in bondage any longer, they were still bonded to the land. Irina's family were Cossacks as Vladimir's had been. In her veins flowed the desire for personal freedom that had become such a threat to rulers throughout history. Her thoughts turned to the image of her grandfather with his distinctive mustache that fell to his chest. The memory brought tears to her old eyes. She could still see him, in his baggy trousers, smoking the short pipe that circled smoke around his head. Irina's grandfather descended from a chief of a band of Cossacks from the Don region. In 1647, their ancestors swept the Polish Catholics out of the Ukraine, becoming famous for their riding skills. These "riders of the steppes" distinguished themselves through history, and the pride of their ferocious sense of fairness and freedom still beat in Irina's breast.

In a small wooden chest, back in her bedroom in the dacha, Irina kept her grandfather's silk sash and his embroidered silk shoes with the curling toes. On the anniversary of his death, they were taken out and placed on the small altar in the corner of the room. Candles were lit and prayers sent on his behalf. Although this was not traditional, it somehow made Irina feel closer to him. She performed the same ritual on the anniversary of Vladimir's death and could feel him with her even more at those times.

Today was very different for Irina, and yet the same.

Reforms again were sweeping her country and the meeting tonight undoubtedly had something to do with those changes. Irina was accepting of change, or maybe resigned would explain it better. Work was work when one had to eat or feed a family. It mattered little for whom the work was done. "They call for change, but things remain the same; it is only the speaker that changes," she thought bitterly.

"My life has known only hard labor for almost nine decades and there is nothing else but this life for me," she had recently remarked to a young man, a stranger to the village.

This young man's presence in Litski had everyone curious. He asked many questions and seemed to write a great deal in a small notebook. An announcement nailed to the news kiosk in the village square said there was to be a meeting where he was to speak to the entire village this evening. Irina was tired, but she was required to attend these public meetings, and so she hoped it would not take long. With heavy steps, Irina proceeded to climb the path leading to the Ivanov house.

This very path was paved with cobblestones, set during the time of Catherine the Great. As Irina approached the whitewashed house, she noticed that the peeling paint and sagging porch made the house seem weary and sad. Once it had seemed elegant to her, with its thatched roof and wooden shutters painted blue. But the shutters had long ago lost their original color and now the wood showed through in most places where the paint had peeled. The condition of the house was not the fault of the owners however. It seemed that there had not been paint or repair supplies for such a long time in her tiny village. Irina always wondered where the paint came from. She only knew that it usually arrived in a horse-drawn wagon that occasionally delivered other useful items for the farm, such as rakes and shovels. But it had been at least ten harvests since she had seen that wagon. One of the women Irina knew from the village mentioned that it may never come again because paint was not a priority now. Irina knew not to question this woman, for she was well informed.

Stepanida Voljenkova had one of the few highest paid jobs for a woman that was possible. This seemed to set her apart from the rest of the simple villagers. A fact she did little to discourage. Stepanida herself felt and acted as though she was a bit above the rest of Litski's citizens. After all, her grandfather was a distant relative of the Cossack Theodor. The bravery of this man of the steppes was legendary, and Stepanida had assumed his implied authority. Therefore, she carried her head high when she came across those she felt were beneath her station. The shy compliant Irina had no concept of the politics that had kept her life one of struggle and pain, and readily accepted explanations given by others as she continued to live each day performing what was necessary to survive.

This day was drawing to a close and as Irina reached the sagging pillars of the once proud manor house, she paused, reflecting on her surroundings. She gazed over fields she had known since childhood. The old woman loved this endless open land where horizon and sky met without impediment. The vast sky was now the warm golden red that Irina never tired of seeing. "Yes," she thought, "this life has been good. It has not been easy, but it has been good."

Entering the Ivanov home, where all town meetings took place, Irina's eyes adjusted to the dim lighting. Without electricity, the illumination came from kerosene lamps that lit the broad, passive faces of her neighbors. Silently waiting to hear the reason for this meeting, they were all anxious to get it over with. Irina nodded to some of them and took a seat at the end of a row, near the middle of the room.

It was hot in this room and almost everyone had heavy clothing on, so it was only a matter of time before things became uncomfortable. The villagers were restless and many of the men were annoyed to have been brought in early from the fields for yet another meeting. It seemed that these meetings never resulted in anything that really concerned their lives directly. Nothing had altered, despite the efforts of the young speakers who seemed to change every few months and each time promised something different. The farm machinery lay rusting in the fields due to lack of replacement parts from Moscow. There was still no pipe for irrigation in the fields and the hope for late summer rains had passed. The size of the farm had grown and shrunk over the years with each revolution or change of power. The peasants, although now free, were still not permitted to purchase the plots they had been working for generations. Not that it would have done any good; they had no money to purchase the barest of essentials, let alone a plot of land.

Irina sat patiently, with the timeless look of resignation and weariness that seemed to be the mask of all Russian peasant women. There was no bitterness, only acceptance in her broad features. Irina had no complaints about her life; her only thoughts now were of being home and putting her feet up. Slightly bored, and looking around at the group assembled in this tiny, hot room, she tried to read the faces of her neighbors. There were only a few women present. Single women, like Irina, were tolerated at these meetings, although not for their input. Their presence, however, was accepted as heads of their families since their men were gone. But not all the women were widows—some were simply alone. No one knew what had happened to their men. In cases, like Sonia Malinoff, for example, they simply woke up one day to find strange men standing in front of their homes, taking their husbands away in large, open trucks. These men were never to be seen again. There were those in the room who, many years ago, had lost fathers, sons, nephews, and other male members of their families in this manner, and no one ever dared to mention their names again. In whispered voices, the memories of those days and the word "gulag" was enough to make everyone fear everyone else, and did much to destroy the sense of community that one would expect in a small village. To have a sense of community, one needed trust in their fellow man and that was something that had not been a part of the village of Litski in many years. The result was that people kept to themselves and only spoke to trusted friends of what was in their thoughts.

This attitude of mistrust had been part of Irina's life for as many years as she could remember. Never knowing who was to be trusted had created a feeling of isolation among the citizens of the once powerful Soviet Union. There was turmoil in the cities, Irina had been told at the last meeting. The change from a socialist government to a capitalist society was creating serious problems. The decades-old effects of an inefficient bureaucracy, nepotism and perhaps worst of all the numbing of the human spirit created by the absence of individual freedom, all played a part in the demise of Irina's government's structure. How this latest upheaval would influence Irina remained to be seen.

Scarcely lifting her eyes, Irina sat patiently. Although uncomfortably warm in this drab room, filled with those whose families and stories she had known all her life, it never occurred to her to complain. As her thoughts began to wander, Irina shifted in her chair and settled her large, sturdy body into a less painful position. Lately her legs and feet had begun turning purple and she imagined it was getting close to her time to join Vladimir. In the meantime, she would wait patiently for the next morning that would grant her one more day to work in her garden.

Just as Irina was about to drift off into a short nap, there was a crash as the door opened and slammed shut. Abruptly awakened, Irina was a bit confused as to where she was and tried to collect her thoughts. In a matter of moments, she realized again why she was sitting in this once elegant room now stripped of its fine furnishings. For a few seconds before the reality settled in, Irina was frightened at the thought of being caught in the home of an official without permission. Immediately, however, she noticed the walls, now streaked and dirty and the bare wood floor with its threadbare Persian carpet and breathed a sigh of relief. Boot steps shook the floors and walls of the house as a young man, followed by a woman, walked through the room and up to the front. Irina recognized the young man who had been in the village the week before asking questions, with his little notebook in hand. The woman was young, perhaps thirty years old or less. Irina estimated her age as being close to that of dear Elizabeta, her grandson's wife.

This young girl, curiously wore her hair in a village style, braided and wrapped around her head. Irina thought this was unusual, since her clothing was not from the region. As the young woman removed her coat and gloves, Irina noticed that her hands were not the hands of a worker. Even at the tender age of thirty, the women in Irina's village showed the telltale signs of working the land on their hands. This woman had long, thin, elegant fingers, and her fingernails were painted bright red, further identifying their idleness. Her dress was of a material that Irina could not identify, but she surely knew it was not the coarse cotton of the local villagers. Irina normally would not pay any attention to either clothing or hairstyle. However, this woman reminded Irina of someone she once knew, a memory that made Irina wary of her immediately.

The young man who had entered the room with the woman now began to speak. Irina had been so busy taking note of the young lady that she did not notice the young man as he set up a large pad of paper and placed a map on the wall. Sensing that this meeting might be more important than previous ones, Irina sat up straight in her chair. Craning her large neck to see between the shoulders of the men in front of her, Irina kept her eyes fixed on the young woman, even as the man began to speak. His voice had the cadence of music as he spoke in polished Russian, with an elegance she had not heard in years.

He told the assembled group that his name was Sergei. Irina noticed he did not introduce the young woman, but continued to speak. He pointed with a stick to a place on the map, near a blue wavy line and said that there was the spot where their village was. Then he pointed to the wavy blue line and said, "This is the river." He then moved his arm a short way straight up and said, "This is the area we are going to be talking about."

It appeared to be quite close to the river from Irina's position. She could not quite follow his confusing speech with words like "20 degrees south and 15 degrees east," and she noticed many of villagers were losing interest as well. Their knowledge was limited to crops, seasons, weather patterns and little else. Aside from knowing the exact amount of cabbages and potatoes that were stored away for winter and how many of them were apt to be taken away in trucks to supply the cities, there was little interest in other matters. Irina sighed and sat back once more in her chair, preparing for another boring, endless meeting that would accomplish nothing. If not for Sergei's elegant speech, Irina would have gladly allowed herself to doze off again.

Sergei continued to show the villagers various points on the map and further explained his reason for being in the village and the many questions he had been asking. He said that his "employer had taken steps necessary to purchase a large piece of land from the government."

Irina sat up again in her chair. "How can that be?" she wondered aloud. "How can land be available for purchase and yet none of us be aware of it?"

Without realizing she had spoken her thoughts aloud, Irina was embarrassed to find her neighbors turning to look at her with surprise. Was this *Irina* who was speaking? No one had ever heard her utter a word before at these meetings and most of the villagers would never have expected her to offer an opinion. Feeling rather foolish, Irina looked at the young woman for an explanation. It was then that Irina realized who this young woman with the braided hair reminded her of.

It was Alexandra Petrovic. So many years ago and almost forgotten, Alexandra. Yes, the nervous eyes, the high pitched strident voice of the young lady, who now everyone knew as Sophia, was the clue. This reproduction of the devious Alexandra sent a chill through Irina and she immediately knew to be on her guard. The memory of Alexandra Petrovic, who had become a Bolshevik and later turned her own parents over to the authorities, came rushing back. Irina knew instinctively that this young woman was not to be trusted.

In a voice that was both harsh and polished, Sophia began to address Irina directly. With her piercing black eyes and painted eyebrows, she could not hide the sarcasm behind her words. "And what do we have here, a businesswoman perhaps? Please, Babushka," she sneered, "tell us your opinion."

Irina could not stop the red flush of embarrassment creeping into her cheeks or the pride of her heritage that also surfaced. She took a deep breath and spoke up boldly, "I would simply like to know how land could be sold to strangers when no one knows it is for sale." She met the young woman's gaze and did not falter.

Sophia opened her mouth to speak, but heard murmurs from the villagers in agreement with Irina's words. From a few nodding heads to whispers that grew louder, Sophia said to herself, "This is not going to be as easy as I thought."

The young man suddenly looked uncomfortable and began to speak calmly. His voice seemed to have a soothing effect on the group and they quieted down. He told them not to be alarmed, that this project for his company would provide jobs for them and that they would be able to earn money without worrying about crops, insects, or weather. They would no longer have to be farmers.

Irina sensed there was more to this speech than what was being told. She began to listen, while at the same time, watching the face of the young woman. After ten minutes of listening to the virtues of their employer, their financial success, their many locations, Irina was becoming more and more uncomfortable. "They are not answering any questions; they only tell us about themselves and their interests. Why won't they tell us what this factory is for?" she wondered.

Finally, Irina could not hold her tongue any longer. She stood up. This tall, proud, granddaughter of a Cossack suddenly had all eyes on her as she spoke. "Will you tell *us*—the people who have worked this land for hundreds of years, first under the tsar then under different governing bodies, all who promised us better lives time and time again—just what are you going to do with this land?"

There was silence in the room. Slowly, the young man began to speak. At once Irina knew that he was going to lie. Perhaps it was the way his jaw tightened imperceptibly, perhaps it was the narrowing of his nostrils. "No matter," Irina thought, "this man is not going to tell the truth, even though he may want to."

"Good people of Litski, I am happy to tell you everything you would like to know, but all in good time since our plans are not finished as of now."

Again Irina spoke, directing her remarks to Sophia, "Then why would you want the land when you are not sure how you are going to use it? What does your employer use the earth for in other places?"

Sophia pinched her lips together and said quickly, "Well, of course, Grandmother, there are many reasons, but none of them are definite. You will see when we have completed our negotiations. And now, thank you all for coming this evening; we will meet again with you in one month."

With that remark, the villagers sighed with relief. Finally, they would get home to their supper! Those at the back of the room, closest to the door, left immediately and hoped they would not have to come to many more of these meetings. The small hallway leading to the front door was crowded, but Irina was no longer in a hurry to go home to her dacha. She had questions that had not been answered. She was still standing when the young man brushed quickly past her, followed by the braided Sophia.

Irina overheard her mutter, "Hurry, Sergei, we must call Mr. Posporov immediately and inform him of the delay."

Sergei answered back under his breath, "Not now, Sophia, be quiet, or you will ruin everything."

Irina was concerned and her natural mistrust of anyone she did not know intimately began to surface. They left the house and drove away quickly, their tires spinning gravel as they did. Somehow, Irina knew, she must discover the real reason these two young people had come to Litski.

Suddenly, Irina noticed something lying on the floor at the front of the room, close to where Sergei had been standing as he addressed the villagers. Irina hesitated only a moment before making the decision to walk toward the object to pick it up. This act would have been unthinkable in the past. Items connected to an "authority" should never be moved or touched. Slowly, so as not to create attention, with her heavy boots still caked with mud from the fields, she inched toward the unfamiliar object. With her head down purposely in an exaggerated characteristic stoop of an old woman, Irina saw it was a folder of some sort, bound with a string and nearly the same brown color of the flooring. In their haste to leave, either Sergei or Sophia had left something behind. Suddenly, there was a light touch on her shoulder. Irina stiffened with fear. She turned to come face to face with Anatoly.

Anatoly looked directly into Irina's eyes with his usual passive expression. In the raspy voice that Irina had known for over sixty years, he said, "So, Irina, my dear sister in law, it was good that you gave voice to your thoughts tonight." Anatoly always carried the sweet smell of the earth with him, and Irina noticed it was not combined with the usual stale odor of most men.

"He must still go to the bathhouse," she smiled at the recollection. The bathhouse had been a favorite place for her beloved Vladimir also. Irina still kept a bundle of birch boughs, near the door of the dacha. The boughs were used to swat the body while sitting in the steam of the bath. It was said that it made the blood flow more easily. Toward the end of Vladimir's days, he would often speak of his wish to "sit in the steam." It had been kind and gentle like Anatoly who carried Vladimir to this communal place during his illness.

People felt free to discuss what was buried deep in their thoughts while in the *banya* with those they trusted. It was a sanctuary in many ways. Once a common feature throughout the region, these structures were less common now, which led to build their own family *banyas*. No one knew where they began, some say the Scandinavians started the practice, others that they were brought from the Asians in the Far East. Many cultures utilized the concept of communal bathing or steaming. The Roman baths, the Native American sweat lodge, and these fast-disappearing *banyas*. All that was certain was that they had been used for centuries as places of healing and open expression.

Inside the wooden buildings, a small stove heated stones placed around it. When the stones were hot, someone would slowly tip a ladle of water onto them, creating the hot steam that opened the lungs and cleansed the pores.

Vladimir would always sleep soundly after a visit to the *banya* and Irina would never forget the kindness Anatoly showed his brother during those difficult years before Vladimir's death. Irina expressed her appreciation to Anatoly, not in words, but in the finest vegetables from her garden. Words were not always necessary between such friends.

Irina shrugged her shoulders at Anatoly's remark and said, "What else could I do? I *had* to speak." Her eyes met his for a brief instant and his heavy gray eyebrows immediately rose. With a look of genuine concern, his eyes took on a questioning gaze. Irina shifted her eyes to caution him not to venture further. Anatoly quickly caught the gesture, in the manner of all people who depend on the slightest nuance of the body to communicate. These two relatives, but also friends, spoke volumes without words.

Irina gradually moved her left foot while they were talking. Her foot touched the object on the floor and when it made contact, she slightly stiffened. She had no business with this object, but sensed its importance. Once again, Anatoly recognized a slight change in her eyes.

"There is a bushel of carrots that is too much for me to eat," she said quickly, hoping to hide her anxiety. "You are welcome to come and take what you need from it." Unwittingly, her eyes shifted to the floor and Anatoly automatically followed them. From under her long skirt, he noticed the corner of the folder and he sharply drew in his breath.

His mouth straightened into a line that said, "No, leave it alone, Irina; this is not our business. This is official property."

Conditioned for years to stay within their boundaries of society and class, fear of the dreaded trucks that would come in the night and take away their relatives, neighbors and friends for nothing more than having a scrap of paper, these two aged people were at an impasse. One, sensing danger, the other sensing even more danger, but from two separate causes.

Memories of the past rushed into Anatoly. When he was a small child, his teacher, Boris Yelenovitch, somehow appeared on an "enemy's list" of names. This man, whose heritage traced its origins to Genghis Khan, was taken from his family and accused of being an enemy of the state. Little did Anatoly or anyone else in Litski know that there were quotas that needed to be filled. It mattered to no one that hundreds of thousands of innocent people were accused without evidence and sent to the far reaches of Siberia. There had been rumors of secret cities where weapons that could destroy the earth were being made. Workers were needed to build these cities and the "prisoners" were made to work from sunrise to sunset in the bitter cold, with barely enough food to keep them alive. No one knew how many bodies were unaccounted for in the frozen tundra of the north, and no one ever dared question the whereabouts of their family members once they were gone.

Irina too had lost many members of her family in that manner. Three of her nephews, many cousins and, most heartbreaking of all, her beloved brother Ivan. Gone into the dark night, there had been no sound except that of her mother, Petra, sobbing for days after the loss of her only son. Irina's father stayed in the house for days, locked in a room with a bottle of vodka.

Irina had memories too, but the promise she had made to her mother that night took precedence over any fear she may have felt at this moment. After the truck that carried Ivan and many of Irina's friends disappeared, Irina knelt by her mother's grieving form. Holding her mother, Irina vowed to her that someday they would be able to fight back against injustice. Petra simply looked through her tear-filled eyes into her daughter's face with an expression of despair that pained Irina. She would never forget that look. They never heard from Ivan after his "arrest," and Petra died in 1945 from a cholera epidemic that swept the southern-most part of what was now the Ukraine. War and famine, epidemic, and revolution were all commonplace events in the life of Irina and her society.

Just prior to his wife's death, Irina's father left the family to join the partisan army at the age of 58. He never returned. His family never knew where he lost his life, and Irina never questioned it. In her veins, however, flowed the blood of independence. The desire for personal freedom would never be quenched. It was with this determination that Irina now faced the man standing before her.

The front door to the house slammed shut with the wind and startled both Anatoly and Irina, momentarily breaking the tension.

"Well, I am glad that meeting is finished!" boomed the voice of Boris, the owner of the manor house, as he entered the room. "I am ready to eat! But first, will you stay, Anatoly, and share a vodka with me? That is my payment for letting them track mud into my home!" He laughed.

"Well, of course, old friend," Anatoly answered.

This was the opportunity that Irina was waiting for. When Boris left the room to get the glasses, Irina once again glanced down at the folder. Without saying a word, Anatoly picked up the folder and placed it in her hands. Looking at him with eyes that said "thank you," Irina swiftly placed the folder under her coat.

She called out, "*Dobra Nocha*, Boris, I am leaving now, with my muddy boots." They all laughed.

With that, Irina left the room, sighing with relief as the heavy door closed behind her. Through the door, Irina could hear Anatoly and Boris begin to discuss the harvest and she smiled with relief.

Slowly, Irina began the long walk back to her dacha. Following the cobblestone path, she heard footsteps behind her and her name being called. She automatically tightened her arms to hold the folder more securely. Turning around, she saw Stepanida hurrying to catch up to her. Irina stopped and waited for her old friend, her heart pounding at the thought of the folder under her clothing.

Although Stepanida and Irina had never been close, they shared many things in common. Stepanida had borne six children, as had Irina. Both women had lost four of their children in infancy. Each had lost their husbands to the same mysterious sickness. Irina and Stepanida had been forced to watch their strong, courageous husbands become childlike, with all of their needs being met by their devoted wives. They watched as the skin hung in folds on men who were once admired for their skill with an ax. The hacking cough, the painful sores, all of these things that no one had ever seen and no one could explain were witnessed by these women. Of course, the Ministry had sent people to the collective to investigate.

The victims of this mysterious disease that debilitated the strong and left the weak to care for them were never given medicine. Irina had called upon the wisdom of the herbalists in an effort to help Vladimir. Although, like most women of her generation, Irina had knowledge of simple concoctions, she needed more than what she grew in her garden. The herbalists were very busy these days and the woman who gave Irina a small bag of leaves to brew for tea was not very reassuring. She told Irina, "I am at a loss with this sickness; nothing I try seems to work. It is very different from what I have ever seen before."

Unlike many others in Litski, Stepanida did not have to work in the fields for the collective. Stepanida had been to school in Kiev and had accounting skills. Not that this was uncommon for someone to have gone to school in a big city, but for a *woman* to have this skill and be able to use it as a livelihood was uncommon indeed. What made this even more unusual was that Stepanida had chosen to return to the village, while most educated people remained in the city. Many in the village avoided her, but she never seemed to notice. Her arrogance alone made this understandable; but since she kept the books for the Ministry Officials, most of her neighbors mistrusted her. In addition, Stepanida had two sons who worked for the Ministry of Agriculture, giving her "connections." This did not help her standing in Litski at all. They felt an odd mixture of fear and genuine dislike, coupled with admiration.

At this time of year, Stepanida became even more overbearing. The Ministry Officials arrived each harvest season and were expected any day now. They would come to take the bulk of the villagers produce to supply the outdoor markets in Kiev. With their notebooks in their hands and their black overcoats, the faces of the men would change from year to year, but the procedure was always the same. Stepanida would walk behind them, recording the quantities and the weights in her black notebook. Nodding with approval or shaking her head at the quality of the vegetables, Stepanida puffed with pride as she examined each small mountain of cabbage and potatoes and wrote the names of the farmers next to their yield. When finished with the inventory, the trucks were loaded by the strongest men.

All of the labor on the outlying farms was manual, since the antiquated farm equipment no longer had spare parts. The waiting trucks would rumble away, and the produce that was left would be divided among the community. Irina would watch the trucks throwing up dust from the road and many times wondered on whose table those turnips and cabbages would end up. Meat was becoming less common and the vegetables no longer had the same shapes or taste that Irina remembered from her childhood, and she often wondered what caused that.

Irina stopped to wait for Stepanida to catch up with her, feeling the folder pressed closely to her body. Stepanida smiled broadly and greeted Irina. The two women fell into step and headed down the path.

"I did not know you had a voice for meetings, Irina," Stepanida said. "But I am also curious as to the meaning of your questions. What is the difference what these people are planning? Surely, it will be a change for the better. Now that we have our new government policies that assure us of democracy, we will all benefit."

"Yes, of course, you are correct, Stepanida," Irina agreed. Thoughtfully she continued, "I am simply confused as to how the selling of land takes place. I thought only the State could own the land."

Stepanida looked frustrated as she attempted to explain to this old babushka that with the new government came new policies. According to

Stepanida, the collective was being "privatized." Individuals could get a piece of paper saying they owned a piece of it, and that meant they could do as they wished with it. Many foreign companies were coming to their country and buying land to use for factories that would benefit the citizens and provide work for them.

Irina listened patiently and nodded from time to time. It sounded sensible enough and similar to her registration of the dacha. She was beginning to think her notions of something that lacked the whole truth were the silly imaginations of an old woman. She began to feel guilty for the object under her shawl and wished now that she had not taken it from Boris's house.

The sun had set and it was now dark and the wind had come up. Both women were eager to get to their homes. Irina was hurrying along the path and, with her cloudy eyesight, failed to see a fallen branch. She tripped and Stepanida reached out quickly to keep her from falling. The folder fell out from Irina's shawl and both women stood, frozen in time, staring at the brown object tied with a string, lying on the ground.

Stepanida's mouth fell open and she reached down to pick it up. "What is *this*, Irina?"

Irina, with a mixture of fear and embarrassment, said, "I do not know what it is." This was the absolute truth of course and her face conveyed that. "I found it," she continued, "and I do not know what it is, but I know it is important to Litski."

She placed her hand out and waited for Stepanida to hand over the folder. Perhaps it was her determined tone, or perhaps their common experiences, or perhaps the conviction in Irina's face that made Stepanida hand the folder to her.

As Irina placed the folder once again under her coat, both women furtively looked around them to see if anyone had seen their actions. Decades of conditioning caused this behavior. Years before they could have been reported by anyone, even a child, for secretly holding papers and passing them between them. Fortunately, no one was there to see them at this time of day. Almost all the villagers were home by now, eating their supper in front of their fires.

As they approached Stepanida's home, the women had to go separate ways. Irina stopped at this junction and with a look of pleading in her eyes began, "Stepanida..."

Stepanida put her fingers to her lips and said, "I will not say anything, do not worry; but please, be careful dear old friend. You are not a young woman any longer and to be involved in matters that do not concern you would not be wise." With that caution, Stepanida turned and walked toward her own home.

Irina breathed a sigh of relief and clutching her wool coat ever tighter, turned in the direction of her dacha. Irina found herself trembling as she entered her familiar surroundings. Wondering what lay inside this brown object, she took it out from under her coat and placed it carefully on the table.

"It will have to wait until I have built a fire and eaten," she said softly to herself. As Irina started her fire, she smiled with satisfaction. Sensing that her life was about to change, she felt an excitement and anticipation she had not known in many years.

Irina fixed her usual dinner of boiled potatoes and cooked cabbage; she cut an onion and a small piece of rye bread and proceeded to eat. Irina's dacha was wired for electricity many years before, but she used only one small lamp. It was all the light she needed since she usually went to bed soon after she had cleaned up the dinner plates and tidied up the large, single room.

The dacha was built originally by her uncle Nicholai. It had been given to Vladimir and Irina by her aunt after his death and after the war, when her aunt had emigrated to the United States. Vladimir and Irina raised both of their surviving children, Kristina and Gregor, in this cozy log home. Irina had been thirty-five when they moved from the tiny shack they had called home since their marriage. She remembered how grand this dacha had seemed to her then. It had two smaller rooms attached to the sides and a large storeroom for all the food she would dry and store for the winter.

The two children were almost grown by then. Gregor desperately wanted to leave the village in search of adventure; and Kristina, then only sixteen, had protested that she was in love with a local boy and should be allowed to marry. The protests went on for months and Vladimir had stood firm. When her brother, Gregor, left to attend school in Minsk, Kristina soon followed. Kristina respected her father later for his protection and they became closer than ever. She ultimately secured a position with a German bank and wrote her mother regularly, entertaining her with stories about Germany and her friends in the banking world. Gregor married and was the proud father of six beautiful, healthy children. The pictures of her great-grandchildren on the mantle warmed Irina's heart. Her eldest grandson Ivan was sure to send more soon, she hoped. Gregor now lived with his eldest son and family, and they came to visit every year. Over the years, Gregor had developed a serious heart condition and Irina was glad to know he was welcome and cared for in his son's home.

Ivan seldom wrote, but when he did, his letters to his grandmother were long and always contained information of the events in his family's life. Ivan's wife Elizabeta was a charming girl, of whom Irina was very fond.

Elizabeta was a professor at the Institute of Science, and Ivan held a position as the head of the Faculty of Research and Paranormal Activities. When Ivan and Elizabeta came to visit, he would amaze Irina with tales of people with special powers. These activities were closely guarded by the government for over three decades, and Irina was never really sure of his experiments. Now that things were more open, Ivan would share them with his grandmother over Elizabeta's objections. She was concerned for Ivan's safety, knowing he was privy to such highly sensitive information, but also knew that Irina enjoyed hearing his stories.

They had not come for a visit in the two years since Gregor had fallen ill. Irina hoped that this year she would see her son and grandson and his golden-haired wife again. Irina straightened the pictures of her great-grandchildren and seeing in their eyes the eyes of their great-grandfather, her beloved Vladimir, she smiled. Having kissed them each three times, she straightened the picture frames and rearranged their positions, as she did every night and morning. Irina was now ready to take her seat next to the fire and explore the contents of the mysterious folder.

Taking it from the table, she seated herself on the heavy oak bench next to the fire. Vladimir built this bench soon after they had been married. Simple and sturdy with a plain design carved on the sides, it was symbolic of the simplicity of their lives. Sharing their dreams while holding hands, they spent many hours discussing their family and the events of the day on this very bench. Many important decisions were made while sitting here in front of the fire.

Irina always felt closest to Vladimir and his counsel in this spot. Settling herself, she carefully took the folder and placed it on her lap. After a moment's hesitation, Irina took a deep breath and then, confident in her actions, began to inspect the package. She slowly turned it over and saw that it was a worn folder, obviously used and reused many times. It was made of heavy brown paper and had an obscure odor. The old woman's fingers were steady as she untied the cord wrapped around it. She removed the contents and could not believe what she was seeing.

There were maps with colored dots on them, photographs of the hills surrounding Litski, and strange-looking papers with little boxes and lines going in every direction. In addition to the papers and photographs, there were some small cards with curious symbols on them. Looking closely through the cloudy film of aging eyes, Irina did not see anything familiar on these papers. Try as she might, she did not recognize this writing. Although she had never learned to read very well, simple words and simple numbers she could manage. She struggled for a long time to make sense of what she was holding, but it was no use.

With disappointment, Irina shook her head. "What was the use of taking this," she thought out loud. "Whatever this means, how will I ever understand it?" Disappointed at the discovery, Irina placed the contents of the folder back and again neatly tied the string. "I will put it back the next time there is a meeting," she said. How she would do this, of course she did not know; but since it was of no use to her, the only answer seemed to return it to its owners—the devious-looking Sophia and the lying Sergei.

Irina took the folder and placed it under the loose board next to her bed. This was the hiding place that Vladimir had chosen for anything valuable they owned. "Now at least there is something in here besides the papers that prove I own this dacha."

Irina got undressed and as she was drifting off to sleep, her thoughts turned again to the folder. The maps, the photographs, the strange writing, what did it all mean?

The next morning Irina arose, as usual, before the sun was up. In the darkness, she put on her sweaters, three of them. If the weather warmed, she would remove them, one at a time, replacing them again as the day wore on and the temperature cooled. Now, however, she could see her breath in the cold room. Irina moved with the early morning stiffness of the elderly. She knew that the stiffness would lessen if she began to move around. Irina ate some *kasha* and black bread for breakfast and made her usual cup of tea. Once again she kissed and straightened the pictures of her great-grandchildren, and then she left the dacha, not giving a thought to the folder that had troubled her so the night before.

It was many days afterward that a bulletin announcing another meeting was posted on the kiosk in the market. Irina heard about the meeting from

Anatoly. He stopped at Irina's home on his way in from the fields as he often did. As they sat in the big room, he began to complain again. He told her that everyone was tired of these meetings, but they were obliged to go to them. It would never have occurred to Anatoly, or to any of the other villagers, to *not* attend a public meeting. It was an opportunity to see one's neighbors as well as not attracting attention. The men who were not at a meeting were noticed by everyone. It indicated that they were not concerned about their neighbors.

The tension in the room began to build. Anatoly did not seem inclined to bring up the subject of the folder he had handed to Irina, but he had wondered since that incident what she had done with it. When he told her of the next meeting, she felt relieved. She had already decided to put it back when no one was looking and forget about it. As she poured tea for Anatoly, she debated whether she would tell him of her plan or not. "I do not want him to be involved," she thought, "and the less he knows, the better."

After making small talk of others they both knew, as well as comparing notes on their great-grandchildren and the other members of their families, Anatoly got up to leave.

Looking into the eyes of his sister-in-law and the wife of his beloved brother, Anatoly quietly said, "Irina, do you not trust me enough to share a secret with me?"

Irina was stunned. She never realized how her silence would have hurt Anatoly! Softly she replied, "I cannot tell you any secrets, because I do not have any." His look conveyed surprise and she felt compelled to continue. "Dear Anatoly, I do not know what the contents in that folder mean. I cannot read the language and all the other maps and graphs. The only things I can recognize are the ravines and the farms in the photographs. There is much more than just the river they were talking about."

"Photographs of Litski? That is strange. Why would there be photographs of Litski in that package?"

"I do not know, Anatoly, but I guess I must try to replace the folder tomorrow night at the meeting—without anyone seeing me."

Anatoly thought for a moment. He was not an educated man, but he could read and write well. "Before you do that, Irina, perhaps I could take a look and see if I can make any sense of things?"

Irina hesitated, but she nodded and went into the little room to retrieve the folder from the floorboards. Irina handed the folder to Anatoly, and with his large hands he fumbled with the string. She helped him to open it. Together, they sat on the bench in front of the fire and began to decipher them.

"Look, Irina, this is Voyitch's wheat field, and here are the fields of Stepanovitch!" he said. As he pointed to the photos of the neighboring farms, Anatoly looked increasingly worried. He turned the maps, first in one direction, then another. Irina waited, as this huge man, with the flowing mustache that was his trademark, pored over each piece of paper. From time to time, Anatoly would grunt with surprise, and at times with concern he muttered under his breath in Ukrainian.

Anatoly only spoke Ukrainian with friends, although it was now allowed and even encouraged. For years, use of their native tongue was forbidden. Most of the Ukrainian writers were imprisoned and the Russian language was the "official language" of the entire country. Little wonder that Anatoly felt uncomfortable speaking a language that he would have been punished for only a few short years ago. Recently, they had learned that Ukrainian was being used for such things as road signs and even being taught in the schools. Parents had taught their children at home in their native tongue for years, but it was understood that the "official" Russian was to be used in public and for all correspondence. No one knew, not even Irina, that Anatoly had a loose floorboard in his home where he kept poetry written in Ukrainian. That was a secret he had kept even from his wife. After her death, he wrote less often, but his heart was in those words under the flooring.

Finally, with a big sigh, Anatoly rose from the bench. He looked at Irina for a long time and then said, "This is a serious matter. I am not sure about all the details, but from what I can make out, the language is very legal and very technical. It seems they are going to build a factory about thirty-five kilometers outside of Litski. There are plans for stacks, which means that something hot, such as a furnace, will be built. The land will be dug up around the river and some sort of holding ponds for water will be placed with pipes leading to the river. I am not certain what this all means, Irina; I am sorry I cannot be of more help."

Irina stopped for a moment and said, "Anatoly, what should we do with this information now?"

Anatoly shrugged "Put it back, as you planned. It is none of our business and we should never speak of it again."

Irina thought the sound of Anatoly's voice was more of a demand than a suggestion, but she nodded her head in agreement. "I suppose you are right; I will replace it tomorrow at the meeting. From this moment, forget what you have seen and so will I."

With that, Anatoly left the dacha and Irina stood, gazing at the maps and pictures once more before she replaced them in the folder. "A factory?" she thought, "I wonder what kind of factory would be built so far from anywhere? But, the young man did say that we would not have to work the fields when they were done. So, they are going to build a factory. With stacks for chimneys..."

As she tied the string once again, she also wondered who it was who sold the land it was to be built on. It all seemed so innocent. A factory was not a bad thing. After all, it could be a clothing factory, or perhaps a factory that made food for babies; or maybe even a factory that made parts for the rusted farm machinery. Irina smiled, thinking of herself driving a tractor, wearing Vladimir's old hat and gloves. She laughed out loud at the prospect of an eighty-six year old woman tilling the fields in a motor-driven machine instead of a horse. This woman, who had never even driven a car! Still laughing, Irina made her cabbage and potatoes, and after kissing and straightening the pictures of her great-grandchildren, went to bed as usual, placing the folder back under the floorboard.

The next morning, Irina rose once again before dawn. As she was fixing her breakfast, there was a knock at the door. Opening the door, Irina let out a surprised shout! "Ivan, Elizabeta, how wonderful, you have come!"

Stooping to enter his grandmother's home, Ivan and his wife disclosed that they had made their sudden trip to give Irina some sad news. Her son Gregor was now with his father. Gregor had died while in a hospital in Kiev. He had contracted pneumonia and there were no medicines available that could have saved him.

Ivan consoled Irina while Elizabeta went to make her some tea. Irina was sitting on the bench, holding Ivan's hand when Anatoly suddenly appeared in the doorway. The four bereaved people spent the next hour saying prayers, and Irina began to accept the pain into her heart over losing her only son. Seated on the bench and while the others were talking, she silently prayed and asked Vladimir to look after Gregor and to be patient a while longer until it was her time to join them both. The comforting presence of Vladimir, and now of her son, both waiting for her, gave Irina peace. But today was today and she let out a long sigh and asked if everyone was ready for dinner.

Elizabeta helped her fix the simple meal and they ate in silence, each preoccupied with their own thoughts and emotions. Loss was accepted with resignation in fact. There was no blame, either toward the doctors or the availability of simple medicines in a society that had seen so much needless death among its people. Irina was comforted by the fact that Gregor had not wasted slowly away as his father had done. For Gregor, it had been a fast entry into the next world. For this she was grateful to God.

After the dishes were cleared, the four of them were seated in the big room, the fire fed and vodka poured into tiny glasses. In the rush of events, Anatoly suddenly remembered this was the night of the meeting. He decided he had better attend and would explain the reason Irina was not there to anyone that might ask.

As Irina and Anatoly exchanged glances, there was the immediate dilemma of what to do about the brown folder. Irina thought quickly and said she was tired and needed to lay down for a bit. Everyone understood and Ivan rose to take his grandmother's arm. Anatoly jumped up quickly and insisted on taking her arm, perhaps too eagerly, causing both Elizabeta and Ivan to take notice.

They exchanged wondering looks as Anatoly and Irina made their way to the small side room that was Irina's bedroom.

Once in the room, Irina had no choice but to show Anatoly the loose floorboard. He smiled as he realized how alike he and his older brother were in their choice of hiding places for their valuables. His loose board was almost in exactly the same place in his own home.

Anatoly, using his strong hands, pried the floorboard up, the rusty nails squeaking as he did so. At that moment, Elizabeta came into the room to offer her assistance to her husband's grandmother. Seeing the two older people standing in embarrassed shock with the piece of flooring made Elizabeta exclaim, "*What* are you doing?"

Hearing this, it was only a moment before Ivan was also standing in the room. With a heavy sigh, Irina told them all to go back into the big room and she would explain everything. Once in the big room, Irina, holding the brown folder, began to tell the story.

Ivan and Elizabeta, both educated, asked to see the contents of the folder. Irina placed the folder on the table and in a short time, the papers and photographs were being passed back and forth and examined carefully. "This is an outrage!" exclaimed Ivan.

"Ivan, we must do something quickly," agreed Elizabeta.

With worried looks, they explained to the two elderly people that the plans were for a chemical processing plant to be built just outside of Litski. The plant was part of a series of units that were to be built all along the river by a foreign company who had purchased the land for far less than its value. Ivan became more and more agitated as he explained that this scenario was being played out all over the country. Foreign companies with no regard for the future were taking advantage of a failing economy and buying land for one-tenth its value. The major danger in this case, according to Ivan, was the holding ponds that were to be located so close to the river. There was no doubt that the river in time would become polluted, further affecting the livestock and those farms that were downstream.

Irina learned from Elizabeta for the first time the results of chemical poisoning. With tears in her eyes, her thoughts of Vladimir's mysterious illness that was new to the herbalists, the deformed babies, and the misshapen produce from her garden all became crystal clear to her. "First it was chemicals in the air, now chemicals in the water," the old woman said, "and the people unaware of what was happening as they lose their land."

Filled with determination and anger, she reached for her coat. The reality of the situation caused all four people to stand in silent shock.

Anatoly broke the silence. "We must go to the meeting immediately!" he thundered.

"Quickly, then, before it is too late," Irina added.

Without stopping for Irina to put on her warm boots and with their coats unbuttoned to the cold night air, the four rapidly made their way up the hill. Knowing the meeting would soon be over, the younger couple went on ahead, leaving Anatoly to help Irina navigate the cobblestone path.

By the time the older couple arrived at the home of Boris Ivanov, they could hear angry voices coming from the people inside. As they entered the house, everyone turned to look at them. Ivan was now standing at the side of the room, Elizabeta at his side, addressing the group. Sergei and Sophia stood in front, next to their easel with its large pad of paper, looking distraught, as they attempted to speak over the din of voices.

As Irina and Anatoly made their way to stand with Ivan and Elizabeta, the room grew silent. Respect for these two elderly people was evident as the crowd waited for them to speak. Irina had never faced a crowd before and was a bit reluctant to do so now. Anatoly, on the other hand, had no problem expressing his views. His voice, strong and steady, asked for everyone to listen carefully to Ivan and then make a decision. Ivan then spoke at length about the proposed plans for the factory.

Sophia, with biting comtempt asked, "What proof do you have of the things you are saying?"

With that, Irina pulled the brown folder out from under her shawl and said, "Here is our proof, your very own papers."

Looking pale, Sophia attempted to explain as the angry voices of the crowd again began to rise.

"We will never agree to this, no matter how many jobs you promise us!" shouted Stepanida. "We are a simple people, but you cannot steal our land! For centuries, others have taken what is ours. They have forced us to leave what we have worked for and taken care of. Our families have been divided, but you will not divide us again. We will not provide you with workers for your factory. We will not allow you to dirty the river." With those remarks, Stepanida sat down, leaving the astonished faces of the crowd to stare in wonder at her.

Irina slowly began to clap her hands and before long, the entire room was applauding Stepanida's remarks. Irina, gaining courage, moved to the front of the room, with Anatoly holding her arm. "Our friend Stepanida has spoken for all of us who care about our land. We will not permit any more attempts to weaken our people. If there is a plan to provide clean water, perhaps a factory that will not endanger our children and grandchildren's health, then we would accept such a factory. If a plan is made to build a school or a training academy for the future, then we would accept such a plan. If there is a foreign company that can explain why our people get sick and our vegetables are oddly shaped, then we will let them build a factory. So, you young people can return to your employer and tell them that the citizens of Litski are united in our stand." Amid cheers and applause, Irina stopped talking. Feeling faint, she grabbed for Anatoly's arm. Ivan decided it was time for them to leave and to take his grandmother home.

Later that evening, with Ivan and Elizabeta fast asleep in the other little bedroom and Anatoly home in his dacha, Irina got up out of bed. On her painfully swollen feet, she made her way into the big room. Without lighting the single lamp, Irina took her seat on the bench in front of the barely glowing embers of the fire. Settling herself, she folded her hands and, as usual, Vladimir appeared in her thoughts. This time, Gregor was with him. Gregor at eighteen, and her beloved Vladimir, looking strong and healthy as he used to be. They were both smiling and, as Vladimir opened his arms, Irina joined him with her last breath.

This was where Anatoly found her the next morning when she did not answer his knock. He opened the door and there, slumped on the oak bench, was Irina Moisevitch, wife of his brother, loyal friend and very brave woman. He kissed and straightened the pictures of her great-grandchildren on the mantle and then went in to wake Ivan and Elizabeta.

* * *

Irina and Vladimir Moisevitch are resting together in Litski's cemetery. It was decided by a petition signed by all the villagers that they would not accept jobs in a factory that could cause pollution problems. After months of negotiations, a training center was established instead. The center offers academic credit for classes in such subjects as environmental protection and ecology. Graduates from the center are now working in all parts of the republic toward a stronger and more advanced economy that will not damage the environment in the land so important to them. A small green surrounds the training center, named in honor of Irina and Stepanida. It is called, "Independence Park."

Valentina

Clutching the brown sweater closer to her body, the old woman shivered uncontrollably. It was attempting to rain again; a steady drizzling rain that was really more of a heavy fog. If not for the passing cars splashing the puddles in the streets and the irritating rhythmic drip from the overhang of the doorway above her, Valentina Sevelova might have slept a bit longer. Shivering again, she gradually uncurled her ample body and turned it toward the street. With the rain keeping passersby to a minimum and the police patrols indifferent in their warm stations, she was forced to get up to urinate. Trying to remember which direction was the train station, she rubbed her eyes to see where she had spent the night.

"There can be no colder place on earth than Moscow in November," she thought. The doorway of the bank building, which was her lodging the night before, offered little protection.

Last night, as all the other nights the old woman spent on the streets, had been a short one. A few hours of sleep were all that one could expect. Foraging through the metal trash cans along this stretch of Komsomoya Street the day before, she managed to find enough newspapers to cover herself, but they were soaked through with the rain of the night before. Valentina pushed the sodden mess of paper away and struggled to her feet. Her greasy, wet hair stuck to her head, the braids having come undone weeks ago. Her once beautiful, shiny hair, hanging past her shoulders, had never been as matted and filthy as it was now. Thinning and heavily streaked with gray, it was once black. In the past ten years, it had been cut only once, by a woman at the clinic, when it was found to be infested with lice. The worker there insisted on cutting it short, over the old woman's loud protests. She wore a wool hat for months afterwards.

That had been over five years ago and Valentina had not been back to the clinic in all that time. It would not have occurred to Valentina to visit the clinic now. Five years ago, her mind had been clear enough to make those decisions for herself. Five years ago, she had not been sleeping in cold, wet doorways out in the open. Five years ago, at this time of the morning, you would have found her in her cozy two-room apartment.

She realized that today was Sunday when she noticed the shops were closed. Sunday was difficult for those who lived on the streets—the trashcans that provided food would be empty until tomorrow. Hoping she would find something to eat at the train station, she began to walk, oblivious to the weather.

She walked slowly past a bakery shop where she used to buy honey cakes for Mikhail and Uri. The boys would shove them into their mouths with glee when she brought the sticky sweets home, warm from the bakeshop. She could still hear their laughter and smiled wistfully at the memory. "Stop teasing your brother, Papa will be home soon!" she scolded. "Stop teasing each other!" the old woman said loudly, over and over again. "Stop teasing each other!" she repeated, in the dull, lifeless monotone of the confused.

Without noticing, Valentina walked through a large puddle. Her shoes were soaked through and barely held together with bits of wire. The cold numbed the pain in her feet and Valentina shuffled along, oblivious to her surroundings. The brown sweater, with its bulging pockets, did little to insulate her from the icy blasts of wind that swept around the corners of the buildings. The bulges in her pockets were leftovers she had scavenged from yesterday's foraging. Half an unfinished sandwich given to her by a construction worker, a piece of cheese from someone else and a blemished apple from the trash can would help her get through another Sunday, especially if she couldn't find anything at the train station.

Under the old brown sweater, she wore her entire wardrobe: a cotton dress, the buttons long lost; another sweater, this one black; and finally two long-sleeved shirts and a pair of brown long wool trousers covered with a wool skirt. This was her walking closet. Her long outer woolen skirt hung in tatters—the wool mending long ago having unraveled. Directly under the black skirt, Valentina had wrapped herself in newspapers tucked into the brown trousers. But, even dirty newspapers were becoming scarce on the streets these days. People needed their newspapers now. They used them to wrap vegetables, to cover old books that were falling apart, and even to write messages. Valentina utilized them for underclothes as well as for warmth. All of these extra layers only added to her bulk as she lumbered along, oblivious to the cold rain.

She had learned how to survive despite the odds against her. "Stop teasing each other, stop teasing each, ea..." she muttered again. A fit of coughing stopped her endless mantra and Valentina held on to the side of a building and coughed in spasms that shook her pendulous breasts. Bronchitis would have been the diagnosis, if she had sought medical treatment; along with open sores on her legs, a toenail that had grown so long it cut into the side of the next one, teeth that had abscessed—all the troubles that neglect created.

Valentina ignored the needs of her body, but more from circumstance than from willingness. Living as she did, eating out of garbage cans and gutters, sleeping in small segments after dark and forced to keep moving during the day, had affected more than her body. As her mind further deteriorated each week, the old woman now roamed the city, searching for food, depending on scraps for survival.

Moscow seemed an unfriendly place, though teeming with people these days. Life in the countryside had become so difficult that hundreds of thousands had come to Moscow in search of a means to make a living. Most returned home, bitterly disappointed. Rumors of a newfound prosperity were groundless. No one smiled. In fact, no one even looked up as they walked. Heads down, collars up, faces hidden beneath scarves and fur hats, people walked by, occasionally bumping into the old babushka without uttering a word of apology. The euphoria of freedoms had given way to the reality of poor management, led by inexperience. The transition to a market economy had faltered badly and there was a sense of uneasiness in the air. Many wished for a return to the old days when government provided at least some things.

Valentina trudged on, instinct guiding her toward the train station on the outskirts of the city. This was a place where the street-dwelling men and women pensioners of Moscow could be found on any given morning. Some of them shared tidbits of food they had found, tossing them into a pot of boiling water set over a small, weak fire. Bits of vegetables, small pieces of questionable meat from behind the butcher shops—all placed into the communal pot to be cooked into a watery soup that would sustain them for another day. Others, sitting off to the side, rocking back and forth, moaning in low tones, in the sorrowful lament of the forlorn. The number of these women steadily increased, with people, such as Valentina, losing their sense of security in the new capitalist system that had emerged in recent years.

The classless society under Communism once provided a measure of protection for widows and the elderly. Although never comparable to the monthly pensions of developed countries, the ability to sustain a level of comfort in one's old age had at least existed then. There were many who would like to see a return to the old days, and it was not uncommon for demonstrations in the streets to cause traffic tie-ups that lasted for hours. Old Bolsheviks, New Communists, and many other factions seeking relief from reforms were becoming common.

As Valentina shuffled along toward her destination, she noticed a crowd gathered a few meters ahead of her. As she approached, wondering what had taken the interest of a dozen people, she heard a voice saying, "There is no use, he is too badly hurt." The crowd, many of them shaking their heads, began to disperse. By the time the old woman reached them, she could clearly see what they had been looking at. Lying on the wet pavement was a small black dog, barely breathing and covered in blood. It was obvious that the dog had been hit by a car and thrown up onto the sidewalk.

Valentina was puzzled; it was unusual to see pets in Moscow. Due to the cramped living areas and the cost to feed them, pets were seldom kept, although mangy strays were common. On close inspection, one could see it was not a young dog, despite its size. The tiny gray hairs around its nose gave hint that it a grown animal who was not accustomed to the dangers of the busy streets of a city. It was obvious that someone had cared for this little animal. It wore a thin blue leather collar, studded with fake stones with a tiny, gold heart-shaped tag. With a sudden movement, Valentina saw a gruff-looking man raise his foot, ready to kick the creature over the curb and off the sidewalk.

"*Nyet, Nyet!*" shouted Valentina as she rushed forward.

The commanding tone of the old woman's voice stopped the man immediately. He looked at the woman in rags, shrugged his shoulders, shook his head and continued on his way. The rest of the crowd dispersed, leaving Valentina alone on the sidewalk.

As she bent down to see the injured animal, her eyes connected with his. He was shaking with cold and shock, and his curly black fur was soaking wet. The frightened dog whimpered as she reached out to touch him. His pleading, soft brown eyes touched something within Valentina and she began to croon gently, "It's all right, little one. Everything will be all right now."

Instantly, she made a decision that she would not let him die. But, first, she must get it to a dry place and examine its injuries. Removing her old brown sweater, Valentina spread it on the wet sidewalk and with a swift move, she scooped him up and placed him in the middle of it. She crossed the arms of the sweater over him and wrapped him like a bundle, picking it up and holding him close to her chest. The little animal whimpered slightly and Valentina knew she must not waste a moment of time.

Not certain which way to walk, or what to do next, Valentina continued to head towards the train station. Crossing Gorky Street and plodding purposefully now, she knew from the feeble whining that the little creature was still alive. Suddenly, she remembered the piece of cheese in her pocket. She reached in with her free hand to make sure it was still there and smiled when her fingers touched it. "At least he will have breakfast," she thought. Stopping at a path leading to Gorky Park, she found an isolated clearing, and after laying the animal down on a patch of almost dry grass under a tree, she hid behind a thicket of bushes and finally relieved herself.

It took a while for Valentina to adjust the layers of clothing and newspapers; when she emerged, she walked over and sat on the grass next to her brown sweater. Carefully unwrapping the bundle, Valentina heaved a sigh of relief when the little black dog began to wag its tiny tail.

"You are glad to see me little one, and I am glad to see you happy," she said to him. The dog was breathing heavily and the blood had dried in its wounds.

Valentina had never owned a pet in her entire life. She looked at the small form with a mixture of curiosity and amazement. Knowing that she must do something to help him, but unsure what action to take, her dirty bent fingers began to caress him as one would caress an injured child. First, she gently touched his head and then her fingers felt for places on his body where pain would indicate something wrong. He lay there calmly, seeming to know that she was trying to help. Gazing into the trusting eyes of the little creature, Valentina felt her heart swell with emotion. It had been years since she felt a responsibility for anything or anyone, including herself. Her gentle caresses triggered a memory of her children and then her apartment, which led to more memories.

Five years ago, she might have even taken the little dog back to her tiny apartment. She would have tended to it and given it love. But, five years ago, she had not been sleeping in cold, wet doorways out in the open. Also in the cramped apartment, would have been her husband, Nikolai.

Dressed in worker's clothes, saturated with the smell of turpentine from his job, her spouse of thirty-five years would have been home on a Sunday morning. Nikolai was employed then as a maintenance worker for a paint factory, where he worked until his death. Every weekend though, he could be found sprawled and snoring heavily on the makeshift bed in Building Fourteen, Apartment 171. The acrid smell of stale vodka, mixed with the turpentine and cabbage from neighboring apartments, was ever present. Valentina would have to be careful not to wake the form lying sprawled on the bed, aware that he could be in another of his foul moods.

Nikolai was typical of many men. He hardly spoke unless necessary when away from home, but found it impossible to hold his tongue in the sanctity of his own house. He would go on for hours, railing at a political system that was grossly unfair and suspicious of everyone. Along with most of his countrymen, he had a love for his Motherland that seemed out of proportion to its inequities. Inwardly he was in torment; outwardly he was obedient. The frustration and turmoil added to his abuse of vodka, and of his wife.

It was a contradiction that Nikolai was a brilliant scholar and yet circumstances had placed him in a menial position in life from which it was impossible for him to escape. Branded a dissident for his ideology and outspoken beliefs in the late 1960's, Nikolai Sevelov and his fellow scholars gathered in weekly discussions about the future. These gatherings attracted the attention of a Party busybody, resulting in his arrest and months of interrogation. During this time, away from his family, Valentina relied on friends to provide for herself and their twin sons, Mikhail and Uri.

Not knowing if or when Nikolai would return was something Valentina had become accustomed to throughout their troubled marriage. Life seemed to be more pleasant for her and the boys when he was away from home. Nikolai treated his wife with more than simply rudeness. It was not uncommon for her to appear at the market with a blackened eye or bruises so deep that she winced as she moved.

Though she didn't understand it, this abuse indicated the illness of her society; like a disease that was spreading undetected, masking the underlying pain felt everywhere. She did, however, understand that Nikolai's problem with vodka made him worse, more violent towards her. And she could see how this kind of drinking affected so many others—traffic accidents and crime were commonplace occurrences nowadays. No, Valentina's situation was not unusual—it was repeated in countless homes all over the globe. Her response was also not unusual. In the classic role of a battered wife, Valentina had taken the abuse, forgiven Nikolai when he apologized, and did little else to alter the pattern of her life. The Russian proverb, "A dog is wiser than a woman because he will learn to not bark back at his master," was taken literally. Working class women had long expected and, in a way, respected a man who acted "like a man, not like a child. "As the wife of a scholar, Valentina would not have expected or tolerated his behavior; however their social position had altered and Nikolai, now filled with self-doubt and defeat, took his frustrations out at home. Though she didn't understand many things, this she did understand and it gave her some patience and sympathy towards him. As his drinking became more frequent over the years, his health began to fail. This only provoked more vodka to anesthetize the pain in his belly.

Valentina was at home the afternoon her husband died. She was sewing buttons on a shirt while sitting at the window. A man from the paint factory brought the news. She simply closed the door when he left and returned to her sewing. Showing no emotion, even during the burial, Valentina went on with life as usual. Their twin sons were not there for the final goodbye to their father; both had entered the military three years before his death. Uri, the reckless one, was reported killed somewhere in Afghanistan, and his remains had not been collected nor sent home. The only information Valentina received was an official letter informing her of his death. She refused to believe he was gone forever; and having read the letter, tore it into tiny pieces and threw it into the fire. Uri's twin, Mikhail, had simply disappeared without a trace a few years before the breakup of the Soviet system in 1991. Half-hearted attempts by officials to trace him failed and it was assumed he had somehow left the country. Mikhail became another statistic among the many missing young men of Russia.

Barely one month after Nikolai's death, Valentina was ordered to leave the little apartment. The reason was simple; she was occupying two rooms and that was considered too much living space for one person. No one bothered to ask if she had any place to go and no one offered her an alternative either. A notice merely posted on her door, giving her two weeks to vacate. She packed her meager belongings, leaving a few boxes of mementos with a neighbor and set off down the street. She did not look back, but began wandering the streets of Moscow, joining thousands of others in the same predicament. In the five years that followed, each day had been a struggle to survive. But Valentina Sevelova *did* survive, and now she was no longer alone.

The gentle brown eyes of the curly little dog connected her with a warmth inside that she had not felt in a very long time. Under her touch, the creature began to relax, trusting her to examine his injuries. Searching for answers, her fingers probing, the woman in rags discovered what appeared to be a broken bone in his back leg and a deep cut behind one ear. When she touched his leg, he jumped and barked in pain.

"Ah, that is what is hurting you, is it?" she said to him. "Well, let me see what I can do about that. But first, you must be hungry and thirsty after this ordeal as well."

Her hand touched the tiny gold heart on his collar, but the letters were too small for her eyes and she realized it was impossible for her to read it. Thinking it was merely a decoration, she ignored it, but left it attached to the rhinestone collar. The little dog began to whimper again and Valentina knew she must hurry. Reaching into her pocket, she crumbled the cheese into small bits. Greedily, he ate from her fingers. Taking a large fallen leaf that had been softened by the rain, she formed it into a funnel and trickled a few drops of moisture around his mouth. He licked it off and she smiled, knowing water was as necessary as food. Looking around her, she found a small branch. After peeling the bark and breaking it to the right length, she aligned it with the leg, crooning softly to the injured animal as she worked. With some yarn from her tattered skirt, she delicately wrapped the stick to the tiny leg, gently easing it into position. When she was finished, she sighed with relief. The makeshift splint was dainty and comfortable and hardly noticeable against the black of the dog's curly fur. She crossed herself in the Orthodox fashion, placed her hands tightly together and said a silent prayer for the bone to heal itself quickly. "If only I had some *oblepikh*," she thought, referring the oil from a bush that acts as a tranquilizer used by the old herbalists in the villages.

Valentina looked up at the sky and noted the hour. She had not eaten and the ache in her stomach told her she had surely missed any food from the communal pot at the Metro station. Thoughts of herself vanished as she wondered how she would feed the tiny dog now dependent on her.

"Must feed, must feed it," she began to repeat aloud. Encasing the dog again in her sweater, she scooped him up and walked further down the path toward the street.

With the brown bundle clutched to her chest, Valentina saw others in the same circumstance as herself. Homeless for many reasons, they wandered incessantly in search of simple things, such as a spot of sunshine to sit in on a cold day. A large percentage of them were in Valentina's age group. Prior to the reforms a decade ago, pensions were paid on time, apartments secured by permits and basic health care provided by the State. Propiskas, or passes, kept things orderly, even though some thought they were repressive. But, without order, everything was more confused, or so it seemed to the elderly. The propiskas had given them a sense of belonging and an identity, and when they were done away with, many felt disconnected to society. Along with the numerous reforms also came privatization. Health clinics now charged what the market would bring and only the newly rich capitalists could afford medical care. The changes started out with great promise, but before long the administrative inexperience showed signs of stress.

The economies in the newly independent republics, who for so long relied on the central control of Russia, were on their own. Most of them were poorly equipped to self-govern, having had little practical training in creating democracy. The influx of thousands who had come back to the central cities, thinking they offered great riches and jobs, placed a burden on all the city services. Living space was at a premium and the antiquated water and sewer facilities were in a constant state of disrepair. The adjustments were difficult for returning Muscovites who felt unwelcome in their capital city. Valentina's good friend, Lidya, had one such story of returning to find a vastly different city than the Moscow of her childhood.

Lidya Kozlovnova had returned to her homeland only six months ago. Born in Moscow, Lidya was relocated with her parents and two sisters in 1964. Her father was an electrical engineer, and his skills were needed in the construction of buildings in isolated areas of the former Empire. Without warning, they were sent to a region near the northeast corner of Kazakhstan. This area was one of three Soviet sites used for open nuclear testing as well as the site of a secret city. Average Russians were unaware of the efforts of their country to win the race for dominance in space. *Sputnik I*, or "Traveling Companion I," was the first satellite launched by the Russians into space on October 4, 1957. The people celebrated the accomplishments with parades, just as patriotic Soviet citizens were expected to do. The second satellite, *Sputnik II*, carrying a small dog named Laika, had many hungry Russians shaking their heads. Little Laika traveled ninety times around the earth, astounding the rest of the world. Millions of rubles were spent in the race to conquer space and another city was secretly built near Baikonur.

Lidya's father, with his electrical design skill, was among the many scientific minds who led privileged lives, unaware of the dangers. Her father saw frightening things during those years at Baikonur Space Center. Many of the laboratories held cages of various live animals, with probes attached to sensitive parts of their bodies. They were used to study the effects of radiation and gravity. Some had exposed organs, such as brains and hearts, with probes attached to them. "Research needs guinea pigs and tortures are sometimes necessary," he was told. He knew, as he quietly discussed these things with his family, that he was taking a risk. However, late at night, he would share what he had seen while repairing something in the Research facility. He always cautioned his wife and daughters to keep silent, and to protect him, they did as he asked. Many of their neighbors worked at the Center, and death from mysterious illnesses began to alarm everyone.

No one was ever told of the accidental releases from the reactor nearby or of the fallout that contaminated the ground on the outlying farms. Lidya's father died, a victim of what she now knew was radiation sickness. Lidya's mother died a year later of bone cancer and her two younger sisters of leukemia. As the eldest of the children, the burden of caring for her seriously ill family had fallen into her hands.

After their deaths, Lidya passed a health examination and began to work in the computer programming department of Aeroflot Airlines. She saved enough money to return to her birthplace in Moscow and faced a much harsher place than her childhood memories recalled. She had a sizable sum of money the day she arrived, but in a tragic turn of events, lost it all the same day. Setting her single suitcase on the ground next to her, with her savings in a pouch inside, a gang of boys surrounded her while she looked at a street map. Jeering and menacing her, she began to run away in fear, leaving her suitcase behind. The gang grabbed it and ran the other way, and Lidya was forced to wander the streets. Helpless and alone, she survived by offering her limited knowledge of nursing skills in exchange for money. She invested the small amount of money she carried on her in bandages and ointments, and soon became well known in the homeless community as well as to health clinic workers. They sometimes gave her free antiseptics and bandages with which she treated superficial cuts and wounds among the street dwellers.

Valentina was heading toward the Metro building when she saw Lidya with her happy smile waving to her. "Why are you carrying your sweater, Valentina? You should be wearing it in this cold or you will get sick," she fussed.

The old woman glanced over to the side of the building. This was where the entrance to this seldom-used section of Moscow's vast underground metro system met the street, separated from the building next to it by a narrow alley. Here, in this alley, almost fifty people would gather at various times throughout the day. At night, it was home to twice as many. Many of the homeless were simply seeking companionship, others a possible sharing of food, and most hoping for word of a possible job.

Lidya nodded in agreement, understanding that Valentina did not want to discuss something out in the open. The younger woman had been concerned about Valentina, hoping only last night that she was safe and out of the rain and cold, knowing how confused she was at times. Lidya knew that most of her friend's confusion was connected with her nutrition. It seemed that the old babushka was so much more aware of things when she had eaten properly for a few days in a row. Lidya sighed with relief when she saw her shuffling down the alley. Moving down the dark crevasse toward the less crowded far end, the women passed Igor Stevicho, tending his fire. Before he was pensioned off years ago, Igor had been a member of the secret KGB and now he was the self-appointed enforcer of rules for the alley. A tall man, if he could have stood straight up, his contemptuous demeanor gained him few friends. He had also appointed himself the custodian of the fire. The main fire in the drum, fed with bits and pieces of flammable garbage, was a most important job. Igor took pride in tending the fire, which was used to light smaller fires for cooking, or for heating water for washing and tea. He considered his contributions almost a sacred duty; for without him, everyone would suffer even more. Besides, from his vantage point at the center of the alley, Igor could keep watch over who entered and thus provide a measure of security for the regulars who called it home.

The fire was weak at this time of day—barely glowing embers—but Igor watched them carefully, so they would not extinguish. As the two women passed, Lidya tossed a small scrap of wood onto the pitifully small woodpile next to the drum and smiled at Igor. "*Spasiba,*" Igor thanked her without taking his eyes off the embers. He knew that in a few hours, he would have to have a healthy blaze going again and that every scrap of wood was valuable. The women scurried past Igor, heading to the end of the alley. Reaching the wall at the back, they went around a large, unused, rusted steel, garbage bin. It had long been emptied of its contents and now served as a barrier, shielding them from the eyes and ears of others. Very few of the street dwellers felt safe being alone, but these two women considered this their private place. From under a pile of cardboard and rags, Lidya uncovered a plank of wood. Lidya had put her sweater bundle gently down and proceeded to pull out two bent steel pails. Each woman took an end of the plank and set it on the pails, making a crude bench. They managed to hide the pails and plank for months, but knew that eventually the solid piece of wood would be sacrificed to Igor's fire. Until that time, the bench would remain their secret.

Before Valentina's mind became so confused, she talked with Lidya many times while sitting on this bench. On it, each shared the details of their lives and confessed their smallest sins to one another. On this bench, they formed a bond that only suffering and desperation can form. Despite the difference in their ages, they were peers now, sharing hunger, loneliness and the loss of loved ones. Valentina, bearing the hidden scars of abuse, once shared the grief of losing her twin sons. On this same bench, Lidya told of delivering her sister's dead child, badly deformed, just before her sister's death. Both women cried many tears on this bench. Lidya, a generation younger, looked to Valentina, when she first arrived, for guidance to survive on the dangerous streets of Moscow; and Valentina felt a maternal warmth for the bright young woman who happened to share the same June 17 birth date as her sons. Today, they sat down on some rags for cushioning, side by side.

"All right now, Babushka, what treasure did you find today?" asked Lidya with a smile as she pointed to the sweater bundle.

Valentina reached down and gently picked up the moving brown package with both hands. Today was not a day for sorrowful memories. This day had brought softness into her lined and wrinkled face for the first time in many months.

Valentina smiled broadly as Lidya pointed to the sweater and said, "*Eta shto*—what is it?"

Valentina placed the bundle on Lidya's lap and said, "Open it."

Lidya slowly opened the sweater and gasped, "Oh, it's the little dog!"

Startled, Valentina asked in wonder, "You have seen this dog before?"

"No, I have not seen it, but I have heard about it. There was a man looking all over Gorky Park for it. Alexandra Malinskaya spoke to him and brought the news to all of us at breakfast this morning. He is offering a reward and she told him that we would all look for the dog. She said the man was terribly upset about it." Lidya had been petting the dog when she felt the yarn-wrapped splint on his leg. "Did you do this for him, Valentina?"

The old woman's eyes filled with tears as she nodded. "Yes, it was broken and it hurt him very much." Tears slid down her cheeks as she realized she was not going to be allowed to keep her small friend. In the brief moment her eyes connected with his, they had somehow formed an alliance. She had saved his life and he had given her something to love. How could she give him up? Her mind raced wildly. She would take him out of the city, far away to a place where no one knew her and the little black dog could run and play. She would find a place where they could both be free.

"Nyet, nyet," she said. "Nyet, nyet, nyet!" Valentina shook her head furiously.

She tried to take back the brown bundle from Lidya, but the woman gently said, "Dear friend, *you cannot* keep him. He *must* be returned. It is the right thing to do. But first, we will make him well while we find his owner. Agreed?"

Valentina became sullen, refusing to accept what she knew was coming. She left Lidya in the alley late in the evening, leaving behind the brown sweater because the little dog was fast asleep on it. She did not return until early the following morning, bringing small bits of food she had scavenged the night before from outside the theater. The women sat on the bench, watching him eat and hobbling on his tiny splint. Lidya told Valentina that the animal did not whine in pain at all through the night and that none of the others had yet discovered him all the way back there in the alley. Lidya was convinced the engraving on his little metal heart tag was in English and that it said, "Pepper." When Valentina called his name, he came running to her, wagging his tiny tail.

"See, he remembers who saved his life!" said Lidya.

Valentina smiled briefly, but with her eyes glossy with tears, she plaintively asked, "Has Alexandra seen the man who was looking for him?"

"*Nyet*," Lidya replied, "she has not seen him, yet."

With a sigh, Valentina crushed her brown sweater into a pillow for Pepper. He went over and immediately curled up on it. Valentina yawned. She had been up most of the night and was exhausted. She settled her large body into a corner full of rags and fell sound asleep in minutes. As soon as she stopped positioning herself, Pepper left the sweater and jumped up on her chest. They were both fast asleep when Lidya covered them with the brown sweater.

Valentina slept most of the morning, and Igor's fire had dwindled once again by the time the two women came walking past him. Valentina had Pepper securely wrapped in the sweater, with plans to take him to play in the park, but the alley was crowded and she had to push her way past the others. Igor looked at her sweater—which she should have been wearing in this cold—with suspicious eyes, but said nothing. Valentina made her way to the street while Lidya stayed and bandaged a cut on someone's hand. The old woman took Pepper to the park, making sure she was on the opposite side from where she first tended his leg. For the next three days, this became their daily routine. Pepper began to hop about and yip with joy whenever Valentina would say, "Play!" It was becoming more difficult to keep him quiet when she returned to the alley, but so far no one seemed to notice.

Each night, Valentina would ask if anyone had seen the man; and each time she heard that no one had seen him, the old woman's heart would beat a little faster. She returned one evening, but before she could ask the question, she gasped loudly. In horror, she saw Lidya sitting down, not on the plank, but on one of the pails! Lidya looked up and smiled her usual bright smile and then nodded towards Igor. Nodding back her understanding, Valentina carefully placed her ample body on the other overturned pail and set the sweater bundle next to her feet. Pepper was stronger now and had learned how to wriggle loose from his cocoon. He began to yip, running in circles around Valentina's feet. Suddenly, he darted away and at a full run, raced down the alley. The old woman immediately jumped up to follow him, but by the time she struggled to her feet from the pail, he had dashed past Igor's drum of fire. Lidya was faster and disappeared out onto the street. When Valentina emerged from the alley, she found him being held in the arms of an older man in a suit.

"Oh, thank you for catching my little one!" she said as she reached for Pepper.

Lidya, afraid there would be a painful scene for her friend, spoke up. "Valentina saved your dog's life and has become very fond of him." Pointing at the tiny splint, she continued, "You see, she even fixed his broken leg." The look on Lidya's face caused the well-dressed man to hesitate. Realizing what she meant, the man gently handed the dog back to the old woman in the ragged brown sweater. Valentina clasped the tiny animal and walked quickly back toward the sanctuary of the alley, leaving the man standing there with Lidya.

He sighed and said, "I think we need to talk, young lady."

They began to walk down the street toward a waiting car. The man introduced himself as Edward Whitehall, a businessman from England. He spoke perfect Russian and so they conversed easily. As they approached his waiting car, a driver held the door open. Edward turned toward Lidya. She had told him the story of Valentina and Pepper, and assuring him that the dog's leg had healed completely and that Pepper played every day in the park with the old woman. She also explained to him that Valentina was confused at times, but that she would try to get her to understand if he would only give her a little more time.

The pleading look on the young woman's face softened his determination to take his property immediately and he said, "Well, I would very much like to have my dog back. I've been looking all over Moscow for a week now and someone told me about this alley. I thought one of the street people would have found him by now, especially with a reward involved."

"They would have, if they had known about him," Lidya said, smiling, "but Valentina made sure that no one saw him." He reached into his pocket and took out a business card printed in both English and Russian. Pointing out his office phone number, he then wrote his home number on the back of the card. He also handed Lidya ten rubles, knowing she would not have money for a phone call. He smiled and told her the money was for dog food, knowing that in all of Pepper's lifetime he couldn't eat the amount of dog food that ten rubles would buy. Edward Whitehall got into the car, saying, "I appreciate your help and know that you will help your friend to understand that Pepper belongs to me. I must be back in London in four days, so that is all the time I can give you. After that, I am afraid I will have to notify the authorities."

"I understand, Mr. Whitehall. I will do my best and I will call you tomorrow." Lidya watched the car pull away and turned to walk toward the alley. She read the name of the company on the business card. In Russian and then in English, it read, Global Communications Ltd. "Ummm, this must be a telephone systems company," she thought. Again, looking at the card, she noticed, just below Edward Whitehall's name, another name that took her breath away. The name she saw was Sevelov, M. Sevelov. "Could this be? What if it is?" she thought with astonishment. Her heart was beating like a drum and she knew she had to speak to Mr. Edward Whitehall very soon.

Lidya reached the back end of the alley and found Valentina sitting on one overturned pail, holding Pepper on her lap. She was carefully unwrapping the yarn from the tiny splint. Lidya pulled the second pail close to her friend and sat down. She reached out to touch her hand, but Valentina jerked it away.

"I know you are upset, please try to understand what I am about to say," she said gently.

Valentina looked up, her mouth twisting as she tried to hold back the tears. "I know what you are going to say. I have to give my little one back to that man."

Lidya nodded. "Yes, but do you know why?"

Valentina, her eyes brimming, sadly answered, "Yes, I know, because Pepper is his and it's the right thing to do. Even if he did let him get hit and almost die!" she added angrily.

Lidya reached out and touched her hand. "I will be back later with some food. Mr. Whitehall gave me some money, so we will eat well tonight." She smiled and left the alley, returning a few hours later to find Valentina asleep with Pepper curled up on her chest. She put the food aside and pulled the card from her pocket, looking at it for a long time. Smiling, Lidya was thinking of the possibilities.

The next morning, while Valentina was at Gorky Park again taking Pepper for his outing, Lidya found a telephone booth. When Edward's secretary told her that he was out of town for the day, Lidya took a deep breath and quickly asked, "Would Mr. Sevelov be available then?"

"Yes, he is," said the nice young voice, "I will put you through."

It seemed like an eternity passed before a man's deep voice with a heavy Russian accent said, "This is Sevelov, how can I help you?"

Just then, the operator came on the line, saying the time was up, and as Lidya fumbled in her pockets for money, the line went dead. Lidya stood in shocked silence as she realized she may have been speaking to Valentina's son. But, first, she would have to be sure. Humming a folk song, she decided to surprise Valentina with a healthy meal and set off to go shopping for it. Lidya returned to the alley early that afternoon, this time bringing some fruit and fish for dinner. Along with some bread and cheese leftover from last night, the two women enjoyed another good meal before settling down for the night.

The next day brought pouring rain to the city. Huddled in every possible place for shelter were the shapeless forms of the homeless. Those with warm clothing would venture out to look for food, but most simply tried to sleep and stay dry while they waited for the storm to pass. When Lidya awoke, she didn't see Valentina in the corner. Pepper was asleep next to Lidya's left arm for warmth, and apparently the old woman had made a cardboard tent to keep them both a bit drier. Lidya thought it odd that Valentina had left Pepper behind with her, but assumed she had left him because of the weather. She reached for the bag of food near by, pulling it under the cardboard. After nibbling a bit and giving Pepper some cheese, she fell back to sleep.

Hours later, Lidya woke up, but Valentina was still gone. Lidya began to get worried and with the rain almost stopped, she decided to try and find her. The problem she faced was what to do with Pepper. Lidya decided to call Mr. Whitehall again. She still had a few rubles left, and hiding Pepper under her coat, she headed for the telephone.

This time the secretary said, "Yes, Mr. Whitehall is in; please hold while I put you through."

Lidya breathed a sigh of relief when Edward answered the call. Hearing his steady voice calmed her at once. He said he would send a car for her and she could look for Valentina, "All over the city, if need be, until you find her."

Lidya was grateful and told him she was holding Pepper for him and would return him along with the car. Within minutes, a long black car pulled up to the telephone booth and the driver motioned for her to jump in. Lidya opened the back door and after placing Pepper in first, she climbed into the back seat.

"Mr. Whitehall will be very happy to get his dog back; he is really attached to him," said the driver over his shoulder. "Please allow me to introduce myself. I am Edward's business partner—Mikhail. He asked me to come and help you find your friend since I know the city so well." He drove off quickly into the late afternoon traffic of the bustling city before Lidya had a chance to speak.

Lidya's heart was in her throat. Seeing only the handsome man's eyes in his rearview mirror, there was no doubt who his mother was. Lidya was tongue-tied as she mumbled, "Yes, I am very worried about her."

"Well, where do you suggest we begin?" he asked kindly. "This is a big city. She could be anywhere in this weather, trying to stay dry."

Regaining her composure, Lidya focused her attention back to finding Valentina. Following Lidya's directions, Mikhail drove carefully in a pattern that crisscrossed Moscow's streets within a few miles of Gorky Park. From north to south and then east to west, they strained their eyes looking for a shuffling form wearing a brown sweater.

Lidya noticed his large hands on the steering wheel. "They are strong hands," she thought to herself. She also noticed, from her position in the back seat, the thick black hair with traces of grey beginning to show at the temples, and the bushy eyebrows above the same soft brown round eyes of Valentina.

Two hours later, they had driven past all the places that Lidya could think of to find the old woman, stopping often for Lidya to ask huddled shapes in doorways who seemed familiar. Mikhail had been watching Lidya's face in the rearview mirror, smiling each time he caught her looking at him. He knew she was extremely worried about her friend, but wondered why she was asking him questions so often.

As Lidya became increasingly frustrated and the wind had begun to gust, she became more and more anxious. He calmly suggested they stop at a hotel for some hot coffee, and get some to take with them in case they found the elderly woman. Lidya agreed that was a good idea, but looked down at her dirty clothes. "Surely, he would be embarrassed to be seen with me in public," she thought.

Mikhail, waiting for an answer, caught her brushing off her clothes and running her fingers through her straggly hair, said, "Any man would be proud to have such a lovely lady join him for coffee."

Lidya blushed and smiled at him, their eyes meeting in the mirror.

Arriving at the coffee shop in a hotel, Mikhail smuggled Pepper in under his coat. The dog recognized him and settled down immediately. Hesitant at first, Lidya felt Mikhail's hand under her elbow, propelling her past the well-dressed customers. Mikhail smiled as he noticed her straighten her shoulders and hold her head high as they were shown to a table. "This is indeed a proud woman," he decided.

By the time the coffee arrived, along with a pastry Mikhail had ordered, Lidya had forgotten all about her appearance and was now focused on who he was. Rather than embarrass either one of them, she had to have more information about him before mentioning her suspicions about Valentina. She overcame her shyness enough to timidly inquire, "Mikhail, would you tell me a little about your business?"

Mikhail answered at once, pleased she wanted to make conversation with him. He was hoping she would relax a bit before resuming their search. "Of course! There is nothing I enjoy more than discussing changes that are coming to our country." For the next half-hour, the conversation revolved around technology that would connect people as never before in the former Soviet countries. He told her all about the Internet and about wireless communication and satellite links. In return, she surprised him with her knowledge of the subject.

Lidya knew that for centuries the means of obtaining accurate and timely information in her country had been restricted to those in power. Her firsthand information was the experience with her father. He repeatedly warned his family against sharing stories outside their home about the Space Center. This early introduction to disinformation and the validity of facts had taught her to be an astute listener. She was intent on discovering any techniques that would bring her countrymen news that was trustworthy. Censorship was inescapable in the past, with biased reporting and alterations of reality appearing in newspapers owned by the State. Events that occurred in one area were often completely unknown five hundred miles away. This false information, designed to influence thinking and to maintain control, was the primary reason for the Russian saying, "Let's take a walk," which really meant, "Let's get out of earshot so we can speak the truth." So it was with great interest that Lidya absorbed Mikhail's technical talk with such pleasure.

As he spoke, Mikhail watched the face of this rather ragged looking street dweller. He noticed how her smile lit up her face as he told her that computers now linked people all over the world with a free flow of information. He was surprised to learn that she had used a computer with the tourist bureau, but only for data purposes. The whole Internet idea was intriguing to her and she bombarded him with questions.

"If you already know how to use a computer," Mikhail said, "it will be easy to show you the rest of the world."

Lidya smiled. She was delighted at the thought of learning something new; but most of all, she was pleased he had referred to a future meeting with her. Suddenly she started. "Valentina! How could we be so foolish to sit here and forget about her?" She jumped up, almost spilling the extra cup of coffee, and hurried out the door to the car, leaving Mikhail to pay the bill. She was in the car when he got there, impatient to get moving. Mikhail felt a bit guilty at having kept them for such a long while, but didn't say anything. They drove a while longer, stopping occasionally to question people.

During a lull at a traffic light, Mikhail asked, "Did you say your friend's name was Valentina? I like that name; it is the same as my mother's." Lidya swallowed hard, not sure of what to say in response.

The rain had finally stopped and the setting sun gave a rosy glow to the drab buildings. Lidya had taken the front seat and was sitting next to Mikhail. She sensed the time drawing near when she could tell him what she needed to, but didn't want him to be upset when he found her in such a sorrowful condition.

Mikhail spoke again, "Please, Lidya, tell me why you are so worried. Surely your friend knows the city well and knows how to be cautious."

"Yes, but she gets very confused sometimes. I think it's because she doesn't eat well. I've noticed that if she eats properly, she seems to think more clearly. She's a wonderful woman with a kind heart, despite her difficult life."

Mikhail solemnly nodded. "Yes, my mother also had a difficult life. It's interesting that they have the same name—Valentina. Yes, I have always liked that name, probably mostly because it was my mother's."

Lidya's heart began to pound. She was just about to say something when Mikhail asked, "Is it possible your friend could have returned to the alley?"

Lidya knew the moment to tell him what she was thinking had come. As she was choosing the words to use, he looked over at her and repeated, "Lidya, do you think she may have gone back to the alley?"

The young woman's mind raced. How could she tell him that the woman they were searching for might be his mother? What if she was wrong? The name Sevelov was not unusual; in fact, in Baikonur she knew of two unrelated people with the same name.

Suddenly, Mikhail pulled the car over. "Lidya, are you all right? Did I say something to upset you?"

Lidya looked deep into his eyes and slowly said, "Mikhail, please...tell me, did you have a brother named Uri?"

Stunned by the question, Mikhail was speechless for a moment. His face contorted and with a tight voice he answered, "How could you *possibly* know my brother's name? Have you seen him? Do you know him?"

"No, he died in Afghanistan, or so they told everyone. I do not know him," she answered, still struggling for the right words. Before he could speak again, she asked him, "Please, tell me about your mother, it's important, more important than you can imagine."

"There's not much to tell of her. She was a warm and wonderful mother to my brother and me, but I'm afraid I was not such a good son. I left home for the military, but I couldn't return to Moscow for many years. In order to survive, I left my post. Weeks had passed and we weren't receiving supplies; it was winter and we didn't even have blankets where we were stationed. It was as if everyone had forgotten that our company was there. Madness had taken over our commander and we were all afraid he was going to shoot us. One night, someone shot him instead, and about twenty of us left and walked across the border. We knew we could never come back and live here without propiskas. I wound up in London, working with Mr. Whitehall; and with the changes taking place here now, mostly positive ones, I was able to come back. Of course, the first place I went was my parents' old apartment, but it had been converted to an office building. Everyone I knew there was somewhere else and no one could give me any information. I did manage to find out that my father had died, but that's about all." Mikhail's sad face reflected his pain and Lidya found herself desperately wanting him to smile again. This was the opening she had been waiting for. Mikhail was finished talking and there was silence in the car. Lidya nodded her understanding and Mikhail let out a big sigh.

He reached for the keys to start the engine again, but Lidya put her hand out to touch his arm. "Wait," she said softly, "there is something you should know." Mikhail looked puzzled, but she continued, choosing each word with caution, lest she be wrong about everything. Before she said another word, she had to be sure. "I have one more question though before I say any more. Is your birthday June 17?"

The big man just sat there, his jaw tightening as he nodded. He stammered out the words, "How, how, do you know all of this?"

Lidya tightened her grip on his arm. "Because I believe my friend and your mother are the same woman. My friend told me these things about her family, *your* family. I believe Valentina, your mother, is the woman we have been looking for today."

Mikhail's mind struggled to comprehend her words. *His* mother? Living on the streets? *Homeless?* Memories of feeling helpless to stop his father's drunken rages surged through him. His eyes filled with tears of childhood rage and frustration. *How could this happen?* He gripped the steering wheel tightly and through clenched teeth said, "You are sure about this? It would be a cruel joke to play on anyone if you are not certain."

"Yes, Mikhail, I am sure. I know your father's name was Nikolai. He was cruel to your mother and she suffered much at his hands. When he died, she was evicted; and with no permanent address, she never received a pension. He left no savings—it all went to vodka." She hoped her knowledge reassured him.

He bit his lip, but finally couldn't stifle his emotions any longer. Leaning his head on the steering wheel, he released a torrent of tears. Lidya reached over and he buried his head in her neck, cleansing years of painful memories with his tears.

After a while, Lidya gently said, "Let's go back to the alley and see if she's returned."

Pepper jumped up into the front seat and began to lick Mikhail's face. Laughing, Mikhail wiped his face and said, "Pepper, let's go, we have to go see a very important person." Mikhail pulled away from the curb quickly, blinking back his tears. The realization that his mother was cold and hungry was almost too much for him. Lidya told him about their little private space at the back of the alley and warned him about Igor's fire drum so he wouldn't bump into it racing down the narrow passageway.

He drove recklessly through the evening traffic and headed for the alley, parking the car slightly askew. He jumped out leaving the door open. Pepper ran ahead of him, past Igor's drum of fire, with Lidya a step behind him. As they approached the back of the alley, Mikhail hesitated and whispered to Lidya, "Perhaps you had better go first and prepare her."

Lidya nodded and went behind the trash bin to their little space. "I just pray she's there," she thought at the last minute.

In the dim light of the alley, sitting on the plank bench, was Valentina. Pepper immediately jumped on her lap and she began stroking him. Mikhail stood in the shadows in dazed silence as Lidya kneeled down in front of her friend and gently took both of her hands in hers. "Thank goodness you are here and safe, Babushka," she said. "We have looked everywhere for you today."

"Where else would I be?" shrugged Valentina. "I found a dry box to sleep in and when the rain stopped, I came home."

Noticing the plank, once again held up by the two pails, Lidya asked, "How did you get our bench back?"

Valentina smiled. "I brought Igor some wood and some oranges to exchange for our bench. Now we can sit and think, just like always." She smiled in a childlike manner, as if proud that she had negotiated and won this small victory.

Hearing a shuffling sound, the old woman looked up to see a large man standing in the shadows.

Startled for a moment, Lidya quickly calmed her, "It's all right, it's all right. He is someone who would like to talk to you." She motioned for Mikhail to come forward.

Mikhail stepped out of the shadows and knelt down. Raising his head, he looked into the weathered face of his mother for the first time in almost twenty years. Their soft brown eyes met and he quietly said, "Mama, it's Mikhail."

Valentina, with a look of recognition and a sob from the deepest part of her being, cried out, "My son, my son!" and began to weep and wail with joy. She grabbed his head and began to shower him with kisses.

Lidya, knowing they would need time to reconnect, slowly backed up and began walking out of the alley, calling Pepper to her. Halfway down the alley, Pepper broke into a run, yipping past the surprised Igor's feet. Tears blurred Lidya's vision and she did not see Edward Whitehall at first, walking towards her, now carrying the tiny dog.

Alarmed to see her crying, Edward rushed to her side. "What's happened? Are you all right? Where is Mikhail? Did you find your friend?" Edward's voice had startled her and she fell against him, releasing her own tears amid the emotions of what had just happened. Puzzled, Edward held her gently with one arm, taking her to his waiting car.

He helped her into the back of the car and listened while she recounted the whole story of Mikhail and Valentina in minute detail. She told him of the abuse that Valentina had endured before the misery of living on the streets and alleys of the city. She related how resourceful Valentina was and how she had cared for herself for so long before her confusion began. She told him how Mikhail had tried to find her, but was unable to. She purposely left out the reasons why Mikhail had not returned to Russia before, but had no way of knowing that Edward already knew them.

Edward listened carefully, nodding from time to time, frowning at the misfortunes and smiling broadly at the outcome. "Well, what an incredible day this has been for all of you," he said.

Pepper barked and they looked up to see two figures emerge from the dim, gray light of the alley. A large man with bushy eyebrows, his right arm around the shoulders of an old woman wearing a ragged brown sweater. The man was carrying a plank of wood and the old woman clutching two bent pails.

*   *   *

Lidya now works for Communications Solutions Ltd. in Moscow, a British joint venture company that provides wireless communication training to schools and financial institutions. She has become part of the sweeping changes in her country, which allow the free flow of information with the rest of the world. It recently started a training program that is offered free of charge and open only to the homeless in Moscow.

Edward Whitehall has his little black terrier back. He recently purchased a tiny white female, named "Salt" and gave it to Valentina as a gift. They often walk the dogs together in Gorky Park when Edward is in the city.

Valentina lives comfortably with her son, Mikhail. She has new glasses and can be found sitting by a window sewing a wedding dress. With a little bit of imagination, we shall let the reader figure out who the wedding dress is for.

Vera

"*Kulak, Kulak, Kulak!*" screamed the taunting children as they chased her down Podorovskaya Street. Even after all these years, the sounds of their words still rang in Vera's ears. Back then, the humiliation of living in Orphanage #54 was almost too much to bear for such a shy child, barely seven years old. She ran faster and faster, her heart pounding and tears streaming down her face. Disoriented in the big city, this little girl from the country ran in terror until her tormentors finally gave up and turned back. She ran until the tears blurred her vision and she stumbled and fell. The teasing of the other children only added to her feelings of guilt for something she could not begin to understand. Looking up through her tears, the frail child saw her first glimpse of the spires of the St. Basil the Blessed, peeking through the trees, in the heart of the bustling city. Little Vera Dimitrivitch felt a wave of peace pass over her as she looked at the onion-shaped spires with their bright colors.

Through the tears of her memories, the elderly woman she had become felt the same peace that brought her here so often to find. The taunting happened many years ago, and now the headmistress could not come and take her back to the orphanage. Vera was a grown woman now, and the painful memories of her early years in the orphanage would not be completely erased. Happy memories, however, were more difficult to reclaim and they were the reason she came to sit on the cement bench.

With tremendous effort, her eyes tightly closed and her chin beginning to quiver, Vera managed to recall a happy time, the time before the nightmares began. Those years when she felt so loved by her parents had faded over the last half-century. Yet Vera struggled to keep the fragments alive, forcing herself to relive them.

Every third Monday of each month, for over fifty years, she had come to this same place. It was a gray stone bench in the park near St. Basils.

From this vantage point, through the much taller trees now, she could still see the nine bulbous domes aglow with color. The tallest of them represented the Savior and the smaller ones were for various saints. It was truly one of the most important sights in Moscow, yet the old woman had never been inside. Vera was like many Russians who felt a spiritual hunger they could not deny, and yet, for self-preservation, were forced to stifle any outward display. Also, like many Russians these days, she did not completely trust a church that had acquiesced to the demands of Communism and seemed merely to be a symbol of the past. Vera had heard that Ivan the Terrible ordered the builder to be blinded so he could never build another one. She often thought, "So many of those grandiose churches are used as warehouses, perhaps it is best he did not see what had happened to them."

No matter the season, passersby would stare at the woman sitting there on the hard bench with her eyes closed. Since she was so close to the church, many assumed she must be praying, and in a manner of speaking, she was praying. Rhythmically rocking back and forth, softly murmuring to herself, she seemed lost in her own thoughts. Over and over again, Vera would ask, "Why? What had they done so wrong that caused my parents to be taken away?" She had asked this same question of many people over the years; a priest, a trusted teacher, her husband Ivan, and others she had met over time, had all been queried many times.

Historically, there were many answers given, none of them making much sense to Vera. Was it true that her parents were "bad" people simply because they owned a few head of cattle and sheep? Was it because they had purchased the bull? None of these reasons could fill the emptiness inside her. Vera had only known her parents to be kind and gentle people, and as she searched her memory for shreds of details, the misty images became clear once again.

The year Vera's nightmares began was 1935. The horror touched hundreds of thousands and Vera was but one small child affected by the events of history. The Dimitrivitch family lived in a place where summers were short but beautiful. Vera vaguely remembered waving fields of grain. She felt the location must have been somewhere in the Ukraine, but without original identification papers, she would never know the exact location. She squeezed her eyes closed and forced her mind to remember again the smell of the hay and the cornflowers in the spring—the tiny blue cornflowers that were the same color as her mother's dress the day she was taken away. Vera could still feel her mother's kiss whenever she stroked the middle of her forehead where Mina's lips had last touched her. She remembered her mother leaning over her and softly telling her not to be frightened and that she would send for her soon.

"Be brave and do as you are told," were Mina Dimitrivitch's last words to Vera and the baby. Was it a baby sister or brother? Vera struggled to remember, but could not recall anything about the child, not even its name. She was not even sure if anyone had named the tiny baby that had recently entered their lives. Vera could remember other children as well, but time and trauma had dimmed them to ghostly images. Were there two older brothers as well, or maybe even three? Vera was never to lay eyes on them again after that awful night when she was taken from the little house with the thatched roof.

As the childhood habit of rocking herself began again, Vera forced her thoughts to think of happier moments to crowd out the tortured ones. Passersby would avert their eyes, seeing the old woman on the bench in her trance-like state. Whether apathetic or respectful, they left her alone. They could never imagine the torment this elegantly dressed woman deliberately placed herself in. Always afraid that the tiny fragments of her good memories would leave her unless she recounted each detail, Vera again forced her mind backwards and relived the painful portions again.

Her mind took her to a warm sunny day with a clear blue sky. It had been Vera's job at six years old to help her mother in the house, while her father took care of the larger animals. When Piotr Dimitrivitch—a thin, soft-spoken man—was out working with the pigs and the cows, Vera and her mother tended the chickens and geese near the house. They had many chickens and their eggs were traded for other things they needed. Vera remembered how the feathers of the geese were used to make pillows and blankets. She would laugh with her mother when they would play and begin throwing the feathers at each other. Her mother would say, "We look like geese now too."

She could vividly remember her father coming into their warm and happy house with the red-checked curtains, his shirt still bloody from pulling a stubborn calf from its mother's body. She could recall her slim, but strong, father bringing home fresh meat, covered with salt and wrapped in cloth, ready to hang it in the smokehouse behind their home. The day he brought the new bull home was the day that changed Vera Dimitrivitch's young life forever.

Her father had been so proud, leading the small bull home from the market. It had taken a lot of the egg money, but he explained that this new addition was necessary for strong and healthy new calves the next year. It was supposed to be a happy day, for it was Vera's seventh birthday. Mina spent the whole day making little poppy seed cakes and many other sweets for the guests who would be coming later that evening. Vera's teacher was even coming! Her two favorite uncles had been invited, and there would be music and dancing. Her father would drink too much vodka and he would sing in his beautiful deep baritone voice. Vera knew when her father began to sing, her mother's eyes would fill with tears at the words of the love songs.

They were a happy family. Vera never heard harsh words between them and the love they shared was obvious to those around them. It was no wonder, then, that when the men came to arrest her father Mina would not let them take him away without resistance. She raised her voice to protest and a man with a black shirt roughly pushed her away. As she began to wail and struggle with the men, Vera heard one of them say, "Take her too." They grabbed her mother, pulling the baby from her chest and tossing it towards someone. Mina began to scream and so did the baby. Confused and frightened, Vera hid under the table. Mina asked to say goodbye to her children first and bent under the table to comfort Vera. The last thing Vera recalled was clinging desperately as the rough hands of the men tore her away from her mother. Helplessly, she watched with horror as her uncles and her parents were all placed in the truck. She remembered it was the strong arms of her teacher that kept her from running after the muddy truck as it disappeared into the night.

Again, Vera squeezed her eyes shut and forced her mind to remember every detail of that terrible night in February of 1935. The color of her mother's hair was the golden brown of honey; her eyes, the clear blue of the lake on a summer day; her skin, soft and always smelling like fresh rain in the spring. No matter how they tried to make her forget that she was the daughter of a Kulak, Vera refused to forget. The word Kulak itself had undergone a metamorphosis in the Russian language.

The original meaning described a miserly dishonest person who made a profit by acting as a middleman and not by his own labor. After 1917, anyone who hired another person to work for them was labeled a Kulak. By 1930, it was used to describe any strong peasant in general. It took on an ominous meaning during the period of the Five-year Plans under Stalin that were started in 1928. The collectivization or socialization programs were almost completed by 1933, but at frightful cost. Vera heard later that over 25 million peasant land holdings had been concentrated into the fabric of collective and state farms. Millions of peasants had resisted the process and chose to kill their livestock rather than co-operate with the government, resulting in the loss of over fifty per cent of the country's livestock. This would take generations to make up for the catastrophic loss. Any strong-willed peasant at that time was looked upon as a threat to the ultimate goal of smashing the peasant farmer and creating a political machine to work the land. Sympathizers to the peasants were termed Podkulachnik and, as in the case of Vera's parents, summarily removed from the area. With methodical precision, in the early 1930s, these purges began. Millions of people were placed in forced labor, and entire families forever dissolved. These practices continued long after everyone thought they had finished. Vera's family was only one example of that.

Sitting on the bench, Vera began to rock again. She softly crooned the songs her mother sang to her as a child. The same songs she sang to her children and now, to her grandson Evgeny. The time was coming when Vera would tell her grandson of his great-grandparents. She would tell him that they had been honorable people, hardworking people, and that he should be proud of them. The current political conditions now made it safe to speak more openly. These things that had been hidden for so many years could now be spoken without fear of reprisals. It was a time of glasnost, openness, and a time for "Truth."

Many people were taken during those dark days. The collectivization of the farms and the need to dispense with potential troublemakers in the peasant population were only a part of the purging. Without explanation or reason, without regard, without respect, trucks came in the night. Innocent people were placed in cattle trains and sent away, never to be seen or heard from again in most cases. The number of people who died along the away was astounding, and an accurate count could never be done. Such was the case of Vera's parents, Mina and Piotr.

In recent years the stories began to emerge and the citizens of this vast country began to realize what had really happened those many years ago. Communication between one part of the country and another was nonexistent during those troubled times. Whether it was a method of maintaining control or simply a matter of economics, the reason was not certain. What mattered was that once a person or group of people was removed from the immediate area, there was no way of finding them, much less publicizing the wrongs that were committed. Even now, it seemed difficult for many to believe that such atrocities occurred in regions they were not familiar with, and many still denied that such violations of human rights ever happened. But not Vera.

It was said that Stalin was probably responsible for more deaths than any man in history, with the possible exceptions of Hitler and Genghis Khan. Frozen or starved during the journey, their bodies would be tossed from the trains onto the vast openness of empty land to the north. The destinations for the human cargo were the camps in Siberia. Camps, or *gulags*, were designated for either work or for settlement, but also for punishment for crimes that had no basis. Cities were being built and labor was needed to build them. It was that simple. In the effort to provide manpower, and in some cases to silence political enemies, the forced migration of thousands was necessary. Little did it matter that families were torn apart, and that the scars of mistrust and the effects of fear would last for three generations. Submission to authority became easier with hunger and deprivation. Those that did not submit easily were silently taken and the profound fear that resulted from these acts could still be seen in the eyes of the elderly generation who still remembered the past. An odd mixture of suspicion and bitterness developed, but the words to express those emotions would never be spoken. Eventually, apathy toward the possibility of creating change took over and the human spirit complied. Vera had learned her lessons well and always obeyed, doing "as she was told."

When Vera opened her eyes, she realized it was time to return to her office. The dismal building of the Institute for Science and Methodology was only a few blocks away, and she had a busy afternoon waiting for her. Her lunchtime was over and she had not yet eaten. With her stomach in knots, she couldn't have swallowed the bread and cheese in her bag anyway. Shaking her head, she wished she had remembered to put in a piece of fruit as well. Ivan had brought home five sweet red tangerines and she frugally had been eating only one each day.

She had been here, on the bench, longer than she had planned and now must hurry to return to her office. Wiping the tears from her eyes and taking a deep breath, Vera stood up—her short, thin body swallowed up in the long silver fox coat. Brushing the coat, she adjusted the large collar closer to her neck against the wind.

Vera was well dressed and took pride in her youthful appearance that belied her nearly seventy-one years. No one would have taken her for more than sixty, which was likely the reason she still had her job. Vera had gone quietly unnoticed on the now-empty fourth floor of the Institute building. She was Lead Statistician, which meant compiling numbers day after day and assembling the reports that resulted. It would have been mind-numbing work for most people, but Vera's accuracy and efficiency had made her necessary to the department.

Her black hair, only lightly streaked with gray, was pulled back tightly into a bun at the nape of her neck. On her head was a fashionable mink fur hat. The hat was a recent present from Ivan, her husband of over fifty years. Vera scolded him for purchasing such an extravagant gift. She knew it must have taken a big portion of their savings, and these days Vera had every reason to be concerned. She had learned early in their marriage that Ivan could be foolish when it came to spending money. They married very quickly and Ivan, knowing of Vera's childhood in the orphanage and the memories that haunted her dreams, had showered his beautiful young bride with presents.

A smile crossed Vera's lips as she recalled Ivan's parents. They disapproved of his choice from the beginning. That he would choose a factory worker, and one without a family, was difficult for them to accept. After the Great Patriotic War, in 1948, the lines of class were always clearly defined. But, Ivan had convinced them that he would have no other woman and the aristocratic family grudgingly accepted his decision.

Fortunately, Ivan had provided well for his family through the years and Vera enjoyed a life of privilege. However, when Ivan was drinking, his spending often became reckless. This never caused a problem before, but now things were very different. The inflation rate was over 200% and money was quickly becoming nothing more than printed paper with no value. Ivan had not been well recently and Vera was afraid that if he required decent medical treatment, it wouldn't be possible to send him out of the country. Deplorable conditions existed in the Russian hospitals. Severe shortages of basic medical supplies were constantly reported in the news, although every attempt to downplay the problem was made. The reports continued to state that the shortages were "temporary," but the situation never seemed to improve. Vera had heard some frightful rumors, particularly concerning children. Poor nutrition invited many childhood diseases to the weakened youngsters and the pediatric wards were always full these days. Sadly, unsanitary conditions and lack of medicine, particularly antibiotics, compounded the illnesses.

Vera shrugged in the time-honored gesture of resignation and powerless futility, and began to walk briskly toward her office. As those before had done in her society, Vera would simply wait until things changed and then accept whatever the changes brought with them. The notion of an individual's ability to create change within the system was still an uncomfortable feeling for most of Russia's citizens. When the thought occurred to speak out, it was immediately stifled. Wariness took over when a new idea was broached, particularly if it came from an ordinary citizen. Open expression was still an unfamiliar concept, despite the rhetoric of the politicians. The flame of democracy was ignited, but Vera was certain it would come with a price. The people of her country had always paid a price when they became too outspoken. Adjusting her collar around her neck, she hurried her steps—steps that were steady and sure. She had walked this same path for many years and knew every crack in the sidewalk.

As she walked briskly, Vera's thoughts turned to more pleasant things. She must shop after work today for the ingredients for the Pasha cake and hoped the line would be no more than an hour. Everyone loved the Easter dessert that Vera made only once a year to celebrate the risen Christ. She loved Easter. It was a glorious time of year and seemed to chase away the darkness in her life. Soon, Moscow would be alive with spring flowers and she could remove her heavy clothing. Vera's light frame always felt smothered in the layers of winter clothes that were needed at this time of year. With a worried look at her watch, Vera quickened her steps and entered the Institute's gates. At only four feet ten inches tall, she looked frail, but was indeed a strong woman for her age. It was that fragile look, but resolute will, that had drawn her husband to the dark-haired beauty so many years ago. Vera was well aware of Ivan's pride that she maintained herself. She often thought, "He is after all a dashing man himself." Although at times his arrogance annoyed her. Ivan had a dignity that was noticeable and he took no pains to hide it. His courtly manners hid the coarseness that only became evident when he was drinking. Vera was used to his outbursts and avoided him during those times. Unlike many Russian men, Ivan had never actually abused Vera. He had pushed her just once. It happened many years ago, before Vera had come to know his habits. She had fallen against the kitchen stove and her small body remained bruised for weeks afterwards. Ivan's guilt kept him from harming her since then. Vera also learned not to challenge his position as the sole authority in the home. She wisely chose not give him cause to be angry with her again. Vera loved him dearly and overlooked his faults as he overlooked hers.

Together they raised two children. Their son Sergei had once been a Party official and was a still a true Communist. With the rapid changes in positions these days, he was now an advisor to the Ministry of Education. Their younger son, Alexei, was a talented artist, recently commissioned to do another rendering of St. Peters Cathedral for a tourist brochure.

There always seemed to be a silent animosity between her two sons, which Vera sometimes found painful to accept. The friction between them started many years ago, when they were very young, and a close brotherly relationship had always been difficult. At school, Sergei had proven to be an outstanding student, while Alexei struggled to learn basic skills. Sergei, with his flair for drama, repeatedly won prizes for his oratory skills while Alexei would get tongue-tied even when called upon for a simple answer. His embarrassment often caused him to stutter and turn as red as a poppy flower. Poor Alexei, it even caused him once to soil his pants when he was seven. Sergei, older by three years, then showed that his cruelty could match his father's as he joined in the taunts of the other children while chasing Alexei all the way home. Vera would find herself indulging Alexei, which would create further problems. Ivan expected both of his sons to be strong, in the way of all Russian men, and kept silent through Sergei's churlish behavior toward his younger brother. Sadly, Vera had to admit that Alexei and Sergei would likely never be allies through life, although she kept hoping they would resolve their differences.

They were only three years apart in age; however, the gulf between their personalities was a hundred meters wide. The firstborn, Sergei, was a tall man with wide shoulders and huge hands. Alexei favored Vera, with a slight build and he barely reached Sergei's shoulder in height. Sergei was quick to criticize anyone who didn't agree completely with him, while Alexei was introspective and gentle. It became clear early on that Sergei was a leader and Alexei was not. Sergei remained single and had many lady friends, while Alexei had chosen a wisp of a girl to marry. Blonde and reticent, Tamara was a good choice for Alexei, and they shared an avid interest in art. Many times they had asked Vera to watch their young son, Evgeny, so they could go to a museum opening. Sergei mocked their lifestyle and interests so often that eventually Alexei refused to allow

Tamara to bring the child if he knew his brother would be visiting. He also confided to Vera that he did not want Evgeny to be influenced by either Sergei's Party philosophy or his boorish behavior.

The home had been split over ideology for many years. Alexei held the views of many artists in Russia and longed for freedom of expression and creativity. Sergei was rigid in his Party lines and refused to compromise. He was convinced that democracy was not in the best interests of Russia and pointed out the discrepancies constantly. "We were so much better off under Communism," he would say. "Look at what is happening since the *West* has imposed itself on us," he lamented.

In many ways, Sergei was correct and it was difficult to combat his reasoning. Things did seem to be worse now than before and showed few signs of improving in the near future. Many government workers had not been paid in many months. Vera herself had not received her salary in three months, but she could not stay at home and really would not have wanted to. Vera loved her job at the Institute. As a statistician, her responsibilities gave her a feeling of independence. Long past the age when she should have pensioned out of her job, no one had seemed to notice. As long as they overlooked her, Vera would continue to go to her tiny office with thousands of files and fulfill her duties.

As with most Russian women, Vera did not know what leisure time was for. Her vacations were rarely at the same time as Ivan's and so they had taken separate vacations for many years. When they were together for more than a few days at a time, he seemed uncomfortable. Vera knew that Ivan didn't drink much vodka when she was with him and assumed that this was the reason for his tension. She was grateful that he could deny himself temporarily for her benefit though.

One vacation was special however. They had gone together to Finland, where Ivan had been many times by himself to conduct business. Traveling to "acceptable" countries was relatively easy for someone in his position. He had arranged for Vera to accompany him on this particular trip to Helsinki. Vera was enthralled with the grandeur of the buildings and the shops filled with goods. Never in her life had she seen shelves filled to capacity and with such a variety of choice. In typical Russian style, Vera and Ivan brought a large amount of money and spent every ruble on new shirts, shoes, electronic items and many things that could only be purchased outside of their country. It was normal for traveling Russians to do this and return home laden with gifts for friends and family. Vera wanted to see so much, but they had very little time on the travel pass they had been issued. Shopping was the goal, not touring. Sergei usually accompanied his father when he traveled. With his position in the Duma, he was given travel passes often and shared them readily with his father. Vera knew that her poor Alexei would not benefit from his older brother's largess. She had tried to talk to Sergei about giving Tamara and Alexei a travel pass for a honeymoon, but Sergei refused. "Do you want him to stay in Finland and not return?" he asked.

From the corner, reading his newspaper, Ivan agreed with his son, adding, "You never know what those artists will do."

Vera acquiesced, not because she agreed, but rather because Ivan had spoken. The subject was closed and Vera would not broach it again.

Hanging her coat up in her office, Vera began to sort through the piles of papers on her desk. She was in charge of compiling state statistics for everything imaginable. Although Vera often wondered what happened to these statistics when she was finished with them, she had never asked. She assumed they were used by the various departments of the Institute in some manner. How and what they did with them was not her concern; she had her job to do and did not venture beyond it. It would not have made any difference if she had known that mountains of statistical information like this were stored in boxes and files all over Russia and nothing was ever done with them.

Today the assignment was the same as every other day. She removed a big metal clip from the top of the pile and barely glanced at the subject on the title page. She hardly ever noticed anything except the columns of numbers that had to be taken from each page of the report. These numbers were then added together and entered on another form. From there, that form had to be combined with five other forms, using the same numbers taken from the original reports. Each report came from a different region of the country and was compiled from other reports from each oblast or region. The work was redundant, but it took her mind away from other things and Vera soon became lost in the sea of papers and numbers. She carefully removed a staple, bending it back to be reused, and set it aside. Next, she took the thicker blue cover page and set it aside without reading it. She would replace it when her work was finished.

In typical Russian style, most of the work took four people to do what one person could have done. The report that Vera was working on had already been through many hands and many departments before it reached her desk. Each step of the procedure involved separate pieces of the report, while the numerical portion was reserved for the statistician. In most cases this was either Vera or her young, inexperienced assistant, Tanya Lebved.

Tanya was nice enough, but given to vague illnesses that Vera was certain were fabricated. Tanya always had too many excuses to leave work early or come in late. Vera also noticed that various men would meet her after work. Most of these men looked nervous and dirty. Vera wondered why this slim, attractive young woman would associate with these types, but kept her opinions to herself. Efficient, elegant Vera quietly disapproved of Tanya's habits, but was most concerned about the health of her young associate. Tanya had developed a nagging cough lately and seemed to be losing weight.

Vera was conscientious in her work and would never let anything leave her office unless it was perfect. Her skill with numbers made this easy and she often hummed a folk song while she worked. For Vera, her job was an escape from the conflicts in her life. She was respected as a meticulous worker and never looked for excuses to leave early as would so many of the younger staff. She always had a smile for the infrequent person passing by her office and her co-workers found her to be more than willing to answer questions, even when surrounded by stacks of reports.

Vera barely glanced at the text portion of the report and began to fill in the figures on the open form in front of her. In her tiny handwriting, she placed the numbers in the appropriate columns. Using her old adding machine, she totaled the figures. Normally, these figures only went to four places. However, Vera raised her eyebrows in surprise at the total she was seeing. "Something is wrong," she said aloud. Once again, Vera went through the figures and rechecked each one carefully. Then she pulled the lever handle on the old adding machine. Again, the same total appeared. Exasperated, Vera decided to check the accuracy of the antique machine. She entered some simple addition numbers and pulled the handle. The answer was correct. Realizing there was no mechanical problem, she went through each number again and watched in wonder as the same six-figure total appeared on the tape.

"Why would the total be so high," she wondered. What statistical analysis could produce a number as large as this? Vera shuffled through the papers on her desk until she found the one she was looking for. The title page of the report read, "Incidence of Reported Cases of Acquired

Immune Deficiency Syndrome," and then in much smaller type, "Region 8965," with the name of the Ministry of Health stamped on the bottom of the page.

Slowly, Vera laid the paper down on her desk. She had read of the disease known as AIDS, but the government had reported in Izvestia only recently that there were very few known cases in Russia. In addition, the article said that the ones reported were from foreign origins. In fact, Izvestia had also reported that until travel became common and Western visitors had entered the country, Russia did not have *any* reported cases of this *Western* virus. Vera also knew enough about it to know that it was usually fatal and there was no known cure.

Fear gripped Vera as she looked at the numbers again. If what she was seeing was accurate, the number of reported cases of this disease had increased dramatically. Puzzled as to how to proceed, Vera could not decide whether to simply fill in the numbers and pass along her paperwork or bring it to someone else's attention. After all, she was merely a statistician and as such should do only what her job required. Vera knew the procedures that would follow any disclosure.

First, there would be an extensive review of her work. She would be asked to substantiate all reports of the past six months. This was routine in such an investigation to be sure a worker had not declined in proficiency.

Next, Vera would be required to appear before the department supervisors and explain the discrepancy to the best of her knowledge. Since this was usually impossible unless one blamed someone else, Vera knew this was not an option for her own personal ethics. She had always taken responsibility for her actions and nothing could change that. After all of that, she wondered, "What will they do then?" Probably nothing, was the answer. She would be told that someone would "take care of it" and the matter would be closed. Unless they did not want the information known. In that case, she would be dismissed and descredited.

Shifting her concerns to her job security, Vera frowned slightly. This was another matter entirely. Without an awareness of HIV or AIDS, the numbers had no significance to her. However, to be different, to stand out even in the most minor way, meant scrutiny. Not only did Vera enjoy her position at the Institute, it provided security.

During the transition to a market economy, the country had suffered and so had its people. While the shops now had large selections of goods, the prices had risen dramatically. The long lines were no longer seen, but everyone knew it was because few could afford to buy what was offered.

Vera had achieved a measure of comfort that few Russian women could claim. Ivan had put aside a nice sum for his family, but it was dwindling fast. Vera learned to be cautious when making unnecessary purchases over the last few years. Along with continuing to work unnoticed past the normal retirement age, Vera considered herself quite fortunate and had an unblemished record. She would have to think about this report before she made an issue of it. She placed the troublesome folder in the bottom drawer of her desk, and using the small brass key attached to a paper clip, she locked the drawer.

Just then, she heard the now-familiar sound of Tanya's hacking cough coming down the hallway. Vera automatically looked at her watch. "Ten minutes late again," she thought.

The door opened and a breathless Tanya softly said, "I am so sorry. I was detained by a friend."

"Not at all child; in fact, I returned early. You still have a few minutes," Vera replied gently. Both women knew it was a lie, but Vera couldn't help feeling a maternal concern for this frail young woman despite her annoying habits.

The fondness Vera felt for her young assistant sprang from a long-held desire to have a daughter. Although both Sergei and Alexei had brought her joy as children, as adults they had grown more distant and occupied with their own lives. Such was the case of sons everywhere it seemed.

Tanya had been at her desk for only twenty minutes when she got up to leave for the bathroom. Vera had gotten used to her frequent trips down the hallway and barely noticed her departure. Busy with the next set of files on her desk, Vera lost track of time. Only when she finished the folder she had been working on and reached for the next one, did she realize that Tanya had not returned.

Vera's tolerance of Tanya's behavior was wearing thin and she resolved to give her a stern lecture when she returned this time. Judging from the length of time it normally took for her to complete a folder of statistics, Vera estimated it to be an hour of absence. "This will not do," Vera thought, "she is taking advantage of my leniency."

Deciding to go and find Tanya, Vera left her office and headed toward the bathroom at the end of the long, dimly lit hallway. Walking briskly down the corridor, she approached the antiquated toilet room with its leaky plumbing and rusted pipes. Her annoyance had suddenly turned to worry. Instinctively, she knew something was very wrong.

Vera's suspicions were confirmed as she turned the worn brass knob to open the door. At first she thought it was stuck. She knocked and attempted to push the door, suddenly realizing it was locked. Repeated knocking returned no response from inside. Listening carefully, Vera thought she heard a soft moan. "I must get this door open," she thought frantically. Her mind racing, Vera knew she had only two options. One was to notify her Unit Supervisor, which would mean that Tanya could lose her job, and the other was to obtain another key from the Supply Office. The choice would have to be made quickly as another moan was clearly heard from behind the door. Without hesitation, Vera chose to get another key.

She had to climb three flights of stairs, since the lift had not operated in years and the Supply Office was on the top floor of the building. As she climbed, she hoped that a long explanation would not be needed for stern Marina, the new Supply Officer. Vera climbed the second flight of steps, resting occasionally for a moment to catch her breath. By the time she reached the office of Marina Petrovich, Vera had formulated her story. "Pardon me, Madame Petrovich, I must apologize for the interruption. It seems I have left my keys in the bathroom and then stupidly locked them in when I left. May I please borrow the master set of keys?"

"Yes, but bring them back in ten minutes or I will report them stolen!" snapped Marina without looking up from her magazine.

She pointed to the wall and Vera grabbed the keys and left with a pleasant, although stiff, smile and added, "Thank you for understanding, I will return them immediately." She signed the book required for anything that left that office and hurried out the door. Once on the stairwell, Vera breathed a sigh of relief and quickly descended the three flights of stairs.

Returning to the toilet room, Vera with hands shaking, inserted the key into the lock. It took her four tries before the lock turned and the door finally opened. The stench was unbearable. Vera quickly put her hand in front of her face and gasped with shock at the sight of the frail form lying in a pool of vomit on the floor. The young girl appeared lifeless until she opened her glazed eyes and looked directly at Vera. With bluish lips, she attempted to speak, but the attempt resulted in another low moan. Horrified at the sight, Vera's mind could barely acknowledge what her nose and eyes were telling her. The moan and the stench brought her to reality and Vera's quick mind assessed the situation. "The child must be pregnant," she assumed.

Realizing she must return the keys quickly, but sensing danger for Tanya who needed her job so badly, Vera immediately went to work. She wet her scarf with cold water and began to bathe Tanya's face. Efficiently, Vera cleaned up the mess around her with towels from the small cupboard in the toilet room.

When the area was clean, she leaned over Tanya and softly said, "I will return in a few moments. You will be all right, child. It is this way only for the first few months, but it will pass. I must return the keys, but I will be back in a few moments." Again, the frightened gray-blue eyes of the young woman met the clear blue eyes of the elderly woman with the perfectly coifed hair and beautiful tailored suit. Tanya shook her head slowly back and forth, but Vera knew that her ten minutes were almost up and she hurried out the door. "I promise I will be back in just a few moments," she said as she left the room.

Relieved to be away from the acrid odor of vomit, Vera returned the keys and breathed a sigh of relief. "Poor child, she is only pregnant, but this will be such a hardship for her family," Vera thought. She knew that Tanya was the only employed member of her family. She also knew that besides her parents, Tanya was supporting an older brother who was rumored to be involved with criminal activities and an elderly grandmother who had been seen at the rail station, selling trinkets. Another mouth to feed would affect the entire family and their very home.

Vera reentered the filth and stench of the toilet room to find Tanya sitting up, her back against the wall, sobbing uncontrollably. Vera leaned down and placed her arms around her. Crooning softly she said, "See, child, I told you I would be right back; now please try and calm yourself. Can you stand? Quickly now, before someone comes."

Tanya nodded her head. "Yes, I will try."

Vera helped Tanya to her feet and the two women, the elder supporting the younger, made their way back to the safety of Vera's office. Vera eased her young assistant into her own chair, the only one with a padded seat. "Now child, tell me how far along you are," Vera asked gently.

Tanya looked up into Vera's kind face. "I am not pregnant—if only it were that simple."

Vera was puzzled. She knew if Tanya didn't want to have a child, all it would take was a visit to a clinic. "What are you saying child?" Vera asked.

"Why else would you have been so ill?" Again, Tanya began to cry and looking at Vera, could merely nod her head. "Do you want to talk about it?" Vera asked quietly.

Nodding her head, with color coming back into her lips and skin again, Tanya replied, "Yes, please, I need to tell someone."

Vera listened carefully as Tanya described her life outside the office. It was far worse than Vera had imagined. Tanya related how her father's drunken rages had paralyzed the family with fear. She told of her older brother's association with criminals. She told of her babushka who had been forced from her flat and who now lived with them in their already cramped home. The old woman begged in the streets to help with food for the family.

Vera's eyes filled with tears as she realized the responsibility on those thin shoulders. As overcome with emotion as she was, Vera also knew that Tanya's story was so typical of the young people in her country today. The weight of their responsibilities was more than many of them could handle. As a result, drug abuse and promiscuity were rampant, along with the dire consequences that followed. As she listened to the almost listless words that Tanya was saying, Vera heard, for the first time, the words HIV and AIDS spoken aloud.

"Yes, and now I have this sickness, but I have not told anyone. Please, I beg you Vera," Tanya tearfully cried, "do not let my secret loose!"

Vera's mind raced back to the folder in her desk and the ominous numbers. She raised her hand and placed her finger on Tanya's lips. "Shush, now child, I will hold your secret. But how can I help you today? What can I do to make this better?"

Tanya smiled weakly, "There is nothing anyone can do." She began to sob and Vera could do nothing more than hold her and rock her while her mind raced with questions about this illness.

It was soon time to go home and after reassuring Vera that she would be all right, Tanya put on her thin, worn-out brown coat and left. Peering out the office window to the wet pavement of the alley, Vera barely noticed it had begun to rain. She saw the long black car with a blonde man waiting to pick Tanya up and take her back to her miserable life outside of the office. This blonde man came more often than the others lately and Vera noticed he never smiled. She wanted to tell him of the episode earlier that day, but seeing his unsmiling face, she knew he would be unsympathetic. She simply watched in silence and turned from the window. Tanya entered his car, without her usual wave of good-bye. The car sped off and Vera sighed with worry, shaking her head in sorrow for her young co-worker.

Vera glanced at her watch and noticing she had only one hour to get the meat for tonight's celebration dinner, she hurriedly put on her coat. Placing the lovely fur hat on her head, she started to leave the office. Turning back at the doorway, she remembered the papers in her desk and retrieved them from her bottom drawer, placing them in her purse. With a sure and steady step, Vera left the Institute and walked the four blocks to the meat market and then six more blocks to her home on Leninskaya Street.

Tonight, there would be a celebration for Ivan. It was his feast day, the day of St. Stephan. Usually observed only by Orthodox Christians, it was also a day for family and Vera used every excuse she could to bring her family together these days. Both Sergei and Alexei would be there and she hoped her grandson Evgeny and daughter-in-law Tamara as well. Vera's thoughts turned to her family and the preparation of the meal. The salad was ready and the caviar spread on small rounds of black bread. With the accompaniment of hard-boiled eggs and small, sweet honey cakes, all served on silver plates with the huge samovar in the middle of the long table, Vera stepped back and smiled. Ivan's heavy steps could be heard coming up the stairs and Vera knew by the sound of them that he had not been drinking. She heaved a sigh of relief. Perhaps there would not be a scene between Alexei and his father tonight and it would be an evening of pleasure for everyone.

Vera greeted Ivan warmly. This man whom she had loved for all these years was still her closest friend and confidante. Although he was far from perfect, he never failed to show his love and devotion for her. Vera was in the bedroom of their large flat, changing her clothes for dinner, when she heard the booming voice of her eldest son. Sergei arrived with his usual swagger and commanding presence. His position with the current government had given him a sense of false pride that reached arrogance at times. This worried Vera because she knew that kind of arrogance often ended in defeat in the tightly knit groups in politics. However, his closeness to his father warmed her heart. "If only Alexei had that same bond with his father, or at the very least, with his older brother," she thought wistfully. "Perhaps tonight, they will come to a better understanding of one another." This was her wish each time they came together as a family, but it had remained elusive.

Vera was serving the caviar when Alexei arrived, but without Evgeny and Tamara. He explained that Tamara had stayed at home, nursing Evgeny who had come down with a throat infection. Disappointed at not seeing her grandson, Vera made Alexei promise to take some herbs home with him for the child and to bring him as soon as he was well enough. Alexei agreed and the four of them sat down to eat at the elegantly set mahogany table.

The men became caught up in a spirited conversation of local sports and as Vera began to relax, her thoughts turned to the events of the day. More tired than she realized and bored with the conversation, she closed her eyes.

Alexei tapped his mother's hand and asked if she was feeling well. "You look pale, Mama," he said quietly.

She patted his hand and assured him that she was only lost in her own thoughts.

Ivan, immediately concerned for his beloved wife's health, stopped in the middle of a sentence and said, "Vera, are you not feeling well?"

With the conversation stopped, Vera decided to tell of the events of her day. As she spoke with carefully chosen words, all three men listened attentively to her. Vera recounted every detail, including the startling rise in the numbers on the papers in her purse. When she finished, there was stunned silence around the table.

Ivan was the first one to speak. "What does this mean, HIG and AIDS?"

Alexei quickly corrected him, "It's HIV, Papa, and AIDS is a disease that kills. There is no cure for it."

With fear in his voice, Ivan snapped, "Well then, it's clear that you must leave the Institute at once. I will not allow you to be so close to someone with diseases."

Vera was silent as she looked at the three most important people in her life. Her mind raced for the words with which to explain her thoughts. Finally, she calmly reached for a piece of the little squares of honey cakes, her husband's favorite sweet. She placed the small treat on his plate and cleared her throat.

Sensing she was about to say something, Sergei broke his silence, "Of course, Mama, you must agree that Papa is right. You must leave the

Institute at once. There is no need for you to continue to work anyway at your age."

Vera took a deep, thoughtful breath. She looked solemnly at the three very distinct personalities who were waiting for her response. Directing her remarks to all of them, she firmly said, "No, I am not leaving my position at the Institute."

Ivan's eyes took on a hard stare. Sergei, who had never known his mother to dispute his father, gasped. Alexei simply smiled.

Vera explained, "This child needs a friend now more than ever. She also needs her job desperately for her family's sake. I can protect her job as long as I am there." Ivan opened his mouth to speak, but Vera quickly said, as she stood up to her full height, "I have made my decision."

Ivan's eyes now took on a look of pride and he gently said, "It is your decision, Mama, and we accept your reasons. But only if you promise us that you will be careful with yourself. Now, how can we help?"

The balance of the evening followed with discussion of the part each would play in the drama that now surrounded the family. During the discussion, Vera had gone into the kitchen to replenish the coffee. As she stood in the doorway and watched her two sons and dear husband, her eyes misted over. "How lucky I am to have such a wonderful family," she thought. Seeing her two sons, long separated by ideology and personality, now discussing what each of them knew and did not know about Tanya's illness and Ivan, listening intently in support of her decision, made her heart swell with joy.

Alexei spoke more than his brother or father on the subject. "I have some friends who recently returned from an art exhibition in Europe. They brought back some literature passed out on the street by some activist group. I'll ask them to let me borrow it and bring it next time."

Sergei, on the other hand, continued to deny that the disease even existed in their country. He repeated the official statements that if it did exist at all, it had been brought in by foreigners and was confined only to homosexuals.

Ivan's questions were centered on the danger of the spread of the disease. Always at the forefront were his concerns for Vera. "If it is true that only homosexuals contract this disease, then is this assistant of yours one of *them*?"

Vera had moved to a chair in the corner of the room, leaving the men to speak at the table. She had been listening and learning. "No," she answered, "to my knowledge, Papa, she is not one of *them*."

Sergei pushed his chair away from the table and with relief said, "Well, then this girl is mistaken, she could not have this disease after all."

Alexei spoke quickly, lest they all mistrusted the diagnosis, "That's not so, Sergei; there are many others who also get HIV and AIDS."

Alarmed, Ivan said, "Then how do we protect your mama?"

Alexei shook his head, "I do not know the answer to that Papa."

Ivan, knowing his wife's will could be as strong as his and aware that she would not back down from her decision to help Tanya, said, "Then we must find out, for mama's sake."

Vera breathed a sigh of relief, knowing she had the support and commitment of her sons and even their reluctant father.

The next few weeks seemed to fly. Vera and her family had much to learn about the disease that was slowly sapping Tanya's strength. They found that information was difficult to obtain and often incorrect. They discovered a range of treatments, ranging from the latest in medication unavailable in their country, at any price, to quack remedies such as special medallions to be worn while sleeping. As the facts began to emerge, the entire family became more and more alarmed. Sergei was still dubious and questioned every finding, refusing to accept at first the enormity of the problem. Alexei uncovered more reliable information and was eager to share it with everyone. They agreed to meet on a weekly basis where Vera would report on Tanya's worsening condition.

Sergei's position at the Ministry was particularly sensitive. He had to be most cautious while probing for factual information. Due to the official government stand on the issue, anyone suspected of having contact with the disease would have either been ostracized or dismissed. He had heard rumors of co-workers with distant family members who had to undergo testing and then the sudden departures of employees from their positions. Sergei would not jeopardize either himself or his family in his search for information. He did, however, uncover some startling reports. These reports verified the rise in numbers that his mother had discovered. Her stolen papers were copied and placed under a loose floorboard in their home, the typical hiding place that exists in almost every apartment in Russia.

At their family meetings, they shared what they had uncovered. Sergei told them that medications to treat the initial diagnosis of HIV positive cases could only be found on the black market at prices that no one these days could afford. He also discovered that testing had been done in clinics on patients without their knowledge or consent. Tests that showed positive had resulted in loss of jobs and even apartments. In some cases, suspected cases of those who had died at home were refused transport to a funeral home or cemetery. Victims of the virus were also sent to "tuberculosis" sanatoria for treatment and not permitted further contact with their families.

Alexei had more practical news. Since his circle of friends were artists and other "avant-garde" types, long on the fringe of what was considered "acceptable" by social standards. These were the free thinkers and they did not conform to what was considered the ideal "worker for the state" classification. Repression did not lend itself to free thinking or creativity. This attitude had made them susceptible to discrimination for decades. As a result, the members of this circle had isolated themselves and were wary of those outside the circle. Fortunately, Alexei was inside. He told the family some dismal, but factual information. "Without prevention, this virus can strike anyone," he said.

This alarmed Ivan, who always listened intently with Vera's safety uppermost in his mind.

Alexei continued, "The most common way of transmitting this disease is through contact with blood or other body fluids of an infected person. The most common way is through sexual contact, but drug users who use needles account for a large percentage of the spread also." Although embarrassed at mentioning sex in front of his mother, Alexei went on, "Needles are scarce and they are used many times over in the back alleys of Moscow and elsewhere."

The information that Alexei had obtained came from foreign visitors from the United Kingdom and France. They also told him that a French health organization recently provided a bus, equipped for testing, within the city. They had handed out free pamphlets and tested over 6,000 people in a five-week period until the authorities forced them to leave the area. Nothing was mentioned in the press.

"They are burying their heads in the sand as always," said Vera.

The weeks that followed saw the family meetings becoming increasingly animated. Careful to keep their voices hushed lest the neighbors heard, they began to sift through fact and fallacy. With each meeting, they gained insight into what was being done and what was still needed.

    The news from Vera became more and more depressing. Tanya had been slowly losing strength and although she continued to come to work, her contribution lately was negligible. Vera was grateful that most of the offices on her floor were now vacant. This meant that Tanya could rest for much of the day, laying on Vera's fur coat in the tiny office. Vera had been doing the work of both women, but never complained. She brought in herbal teas to help combat Tanya's frequent bouts of diarrhea. She also made poultices for the spreading skin lesions that Tanya had developed. Ministering to the young girl with gentle touches, the two shared their stories. The tall blonde man came every day to take her home, with Vera helping her down the stairs to his car. They never exchanged words, but he exchanged glances with the old woman, silently acknowledging her help.

    Tanya would never have known what to name the illness if not for a former boyfriend, Piotr. He had died of complications of AIDS less than two years ago. His end had come quickly and was due to pneumonia, an opportunistic disease that was usually the cause of death. It was only a few months after Piotr's death that Tanya had come down with a cough and a cold that would not go away. Later, in a quickly arranged lunch meeting with Piotr's closest friend, Dmitri, she learned the name of the illness that had taken Piotr from her forever. In a low whisper, Dmitri explained to Tanya he had known Piotr's former girlfriend, who had also died of the virus. Shortly after Tanya had fallen in love with him, Piotr had taken ill. Dmitri questioned others and now had a better understanding of the dire consequences of unprotected sex. Knowing that most young men did not wear protection, always excusing this with "they are too expensive," or "the shops did not have any." Women easily accepted their reasons, which were true in most cases.

    After Piotr's death, Tanya began to sleep with other men for the few rubles they would pay her. Not only did she need the money, but she was in grief over Piotr and sold herself without caring about the consequences. After Dimitri told her the whole story, she became even more despondent and decided that even though her fate had been sealed, she would wait for the day when she could join Piotr. Her destitute family had grown used to the extra money, so she continued to sell her body, not realizing that she was placing others at risk with the disease. When her name came up on the list for a position at the Institute, she tried to put the life she had been leading behind her. It was too late by then, the disease had taken its toll.

Vera knew that Tanya would not be able to come in to work much longer. She arranged a short "vacation" time for Tanya through the Department Head to be used when that time came.

To Vera's amazement, Tanya had not yet told her family. "How can you not share with them what you are going through?" she asked.

Tanya merely shrugged her thin shoulders and replied, "I cannot bring them this shame and add to their troubles."

Again, Vera gave silent thanks for the love and support of her own family. She turned her head and her eyes filled with tears for her pale young friend. "How many others are carrying this burden alone?" she wondered.

Two weeks later, while the sun shone brightly on an early summer day, Tanya Lebved, aged 24, died in Vera's arms on the floor of the shabby office. Vera summoned the tall blonde friend who had promised to take care of her body and deliver it to her parents. When he arrived, Vera greeted the unsmiling face of the man who had been driving Tanya to and from work for months. She now realized why he never smiled. Dmitri told her that he had done this same thing for too many of his friends over the past two years, and that Tanya was yet another victim of this dreaded disease.

When he left, Vera sat at her desk and cried for a very long time. It was then that she decided the direction her life would take.

That night, she told her family that the end came peacefully for Tanya. "I am leaving the Institute," she announced. Ivan, Sergei and Alexei all understood her reasons when she related the conversation with Dmitri. "We cannot remain silent any longer," she said. With that, Vera went into the next room and returned moments later with the copies of the statistics in her hands. "Sergei, I would like to go with you to the Health Ministry."

Sergei, knowing his mother would not be swayed and proud of her courage, replied, "I will see to arranging a meeting with the Health Minister tomorrow, Mama."

Alexei offered to provide all the literature he had collected concerning prevention and transmission. "If we can prevent even one needless death, we must do this."

"Yes, Vera," said Ivan, "we will all go with you."

*   *   *

The next day, Vera resigned her position as Head Statistician for the Institute of Science and Methodology. She no longer visits the bench to recall memories from the past and now concentrates on the future. Her nightmares have disappeared and she now speaks out without fear. Her new position as Head Administrator for an AIDS activist clinic, with the help of others around the world, disseminates the latest information available on HIV and AIDS. It is accurate and free to those who ask for it. Along with Alexei and Tamara, who distribute free needles and condoms, both Ivan and Sergei work with a European organization to contact the most vulnerable groups to stem the spread of the disease.

Positive changes are occurring amid a climate that is still filled with uncertainty and fear of reprisal. Vera hopes that increasing awareness of the problems will save others like Tanya and Piotr. In the clinic, along with photos of her family, there is one of a small, attractive young woman with thin shoulders and blonde hair. Vera is happy to tell the story of her young assistant to anyone who asks when they come to visit.

Helena

The security door of the modest white home with its pink shutters at 1206 Elm Place was locked. The blinds were tightly drawn and no one answered the doorbell. The morning newspaper was stuck in the bushes on the side of the porch. Wearing a black, ankle-length cassock and stiff, black *kalimali* hat, both indicating his Russian Orthodox vocation, the thin young man walked slowly back toward his car. He stood for a moment, his hand resting on the door handle. Thoughtfully staring at the cozy home he visited so frequently, the bearded man checked his watch to verify the time. He decided to wait a few minutes longer. While standing next to the church's old yellow Datsun, he noticed that the tulips and hyacinths had bloomed since his last visit. He smiled knowing that Helena would be pleased about that. The fragrant purple and pink hyacinths were her favorites and he knew it would not be long before one of them wound up on the patio in a tiny china pot until it faded and was replanted in the garden. He chuckled to himself, knowing it would be put back into precise position.

Helena gave the words *tidy* and *organized* a whole new meaning. Everything in the old Babushka's life was tidy and organized—a trait she shared with her husband. In fact, it was common to see her brushing imaginary lint from Gennady's shoulder as she passed behind him while serving their favorite Turkish coffee. Even during the blistering heat of last year's Kansas summer, the elderly Russian couple never appeared unkempt. To ensure that look, Helena packed for three clothing changes a day for their recent promotion trips. Gennady never seemed to mind his wife's penchant for order and often praised her for it. He was proud of her and proud of their home. Frequently, he would painfully rise from his chair and walk slowly across the room to straighten an already straight picture on the wall himself.

Helena's need for order and cleanliness undoubtedly came from her early years spent amid the chaos and grime of the uncertainty of war. Escaping those horrors, she found comfort in keeping order in her life. Even the garden showed its foliage to the best advantage. Tiny yellow violas were planted in front of taller lavender foxglove, surrounded by phlox of all colors. There was not a spent bloom on the roses and even the prunings were neatly tied in bundles near the trash barrel. The overall effect was a balance of color, with pink and white dominating. Although beautiful in its form and presentation, it spoke volumes of the personalities of its gardener. Rigid and stern, Helena could often be brisk in her approach to others. She seemed to be erecting barriers around herself in an effort to protect her family from possible harm.

The old Russian couple complimented each other. Helena, with her white hair tightly coiled in a braid at the nape of her neck, and elegant Gennady wearing a chest full of medals on his black suit—they were an almost regal-looking pair.

One afternoon, not long ago, Gennady gave the young priest an explanation of each of the medals. The normal one-hour visit had turned into a four-hour history lesson as Gennady recounted to Father Josiah the details of each war-torn memento. That was also the afternoon he introduced the young man, for the first time, to the manuscript, or "The History" as Gennady preferred to call it. Showing the thick binder to Father Josiah, the white-haired gentleman explained, "You are the only person outside of the family to see this book. When you see what is written, you will understand why." Painstakingly typed on an old Cyrillic typewriter—with news clippings and photographs used liberally to verify facts—the book was a work of art in itself. The old Tsarist had assembled the manuscript after his retirement almost twenty years ago. It was meant to be no more than a chronology of family history, to be given to his children. After completion, it sat on a shelf in the laundry room, pushed back further and further into the shadows, awaiting the day when the children would be interested.

That afternoon, almost three years ago, proved to be the first of many discussions surrounding the events in Gennady and Helena's diaries. Sitting on the wrought iron bench in the garden, surrounded by the grape arbor and the smell of Helena's prized roses, the couple explained the turmoil they had faced so many years before. Father Josiah was transported to the suffering of a country and the courage of its people that before he had only read about. Gennady's vivid descriptions of places and events and his recounting of minute details often drew tears from all three of them as the memories unfolded.

Gennady's recall, at ninety years of age, was surprising and his descriptions, always passionate. Often the young priest felt as if he were actually standing next to him and seeing with his own eyes the advancing Chinese army in the northern reaches of Siberia. He became witness to the sight of six young cadets hanging in the courtyard of a slave labor camp. He too could feel the cold muzzle of a gun barrel pressed against his neck. Father Josiah's eyes filled with tears as he learned of the fear and desperation of Helena when she was also arrested and interrogated by a Gestapo agent.

The old man's thunderous voice would escalate as he railed against "the Evil Communists that still run the Motherland and who claim to have put that behind them now. They destroyed what was once Russia and took the souls from the people."

Helena would put her finger to her lips and say, "Hush, Papa, calm yourself." Only then, the man who more than once risked his life to save others would become subdued.

Puzzled, Father Josiah wondered out loud as he stood in front of the house, "Where have Gennady and Helena gone off to this time?"

It was not uncommon for them to be away from home these days. On the contrary, the elderly couple, whom he had been calling on weekly for the past three years, were seldom in Oak Grove these days. Two years ago at Father Josiah's urging, Gennady had reluctantly agreed to let a publisher see "The History." The elderly couple allowed a portion of the manuscript to be published and had become inundated with requests for interviews and promotion responsibilities. Father Josiah worried that the extensive travel was not in their best interests at their age, but they were eager to tell their story and he did not interfere.

What did seem strange, though, was that they had not mentioned to him that they had another trip planned, as they always had before. "It's unlike Helena to forget even the smallest detail, but I suppose with everything on her mind lately, it is to be expected," he speculated.

Just then, he heard a woman's voice call from across the street. "Father, Father, please wait!" cried the voice. Father Josiah turned to see a plump woman, her pink curlers showing under a yellow bouffant hair net, running down her front porch steps toward him. She was waving an envelope. Red faced and out of breath, she came up and handed him a long blue envelope. "This is from Helena. She said you would be coming by today. I almost missed you, I was watching General Hospital." Noticing his questioning look, she sheepishly said, "It's a soap opera, Father."

"Ah, yes, Luke and Laura," he laughed heartily. "I *have* heard of them. You are Mrs. Kelly, if I remember correctly?" Helena had mentioned that a new family had moved to the block and that they were Irish.

"I hope they start to take care of the front yard," Helena had said. "It is all overgrown with weeds since Mrs. Kozarchich moved." Glancing across the street, Father Josiah noticed the weeds were still there.

"Yes, Father. Helena said the note in the envelope would explain where they went and she also said you would understand," Mrs. Kelly added with an inquiring look. It was obvious that she was hoping he would open the envelope right then and there. Seeing no reason to do so, Father Josiah politely thanked her and got into the car, waving as he drove away. Glancing at his watch, he realized he had at least two hours before his next pastoral call. He drove north on Elm Place and turned east, toward Kowalski Park. This part of town was his favorite area.

It was a quiet, pleasant neighborhood, with tidy houses set behind white picket fences. Long known as "steeltown," this section of the city was occupied mainly by immigrants from countries such as Poland, Russia and other eastern European nations. Most of the residents emigrated following World War II and settled in industrial areas, such as this one, all across the United States.

Bringing their trades with them, they created tightly knit communities. They preserved their holiday customs and assimilated into society while offering their propensity for hard work to the eagerly awaiting factories, who often took advantage of them. They were frequently paid much less than citizens and did not know about such things as retirement plans and extra pay for extra hours. They were grateful to have jobs and never complained about receiving one-third of the wages that others received. Many of these people had acquired their skills by working in slave labor factories to provide war materials and were now experiencing the freedom that had been held from them for many years. They could worship as they pleased, they could educate their children in democracy and could earn an income to provide for them. It was all so different, so new, and they did not complain. Pipefitters, electricians, machinists, and assembly workers were put to work in various manufacturing jobs that did not require proficient language skills.

Their children grew up amid a society that did not really want to look back, only to look forward. As a result, they often resented their "old-fashioned" parents and rejected the lessons learned only by experience. Many, such as Gennady and Helena's children, refused to learn their native language and left behind the "old country" ways, as well as the "old country" memories.

Oak Grove had grown into a thriving city, attempting to maintain its individuality despite the recent urban sprawl that tried to swallow it up. For many years the tall chimney stacks of Edgcomb Steel, belching with thick, putrid black smoke, had identified the city. The government regulations due to the Clean Air Act had cleaned up the soot and smoke, and Oak Grove had become a desirable place for new residential and economic development. Whole new neighborhoods were springing up and thousands of new residents had taken up lives there. The old downtown area merchants struggled to keep their doors open due to the discount stores and huge shopping malls that lined both sides of the recently built highway, luring the one-stop shoppers. The residents of the "steeltown" neighborhood of Oak Grove, however, preferred to do business with Stanislav of Stanley's Butcher Shop, and Nick, the owner of Shear Pleasure Barber Shop.

In these small shops that seemed to have been there forever, they felt at home. The familiar faces of friends were welcome and they could even catch up with some gossip while patiently waiting to be served. Their children preferred the mega-malls, with designer shops that all carried the same merchandise, but the elderly residents of Oak Grove kept their dwindling numbers within the protective circle of trusted neighbors.

Father Josiah turned north on Main Street and thought, "What a perfect time of day to sit by the lake to read Helena's letter." The park was beautiful at this time of year and the ducks on the lake knew him well. He reached back to the floor behind the passenger seat and felt for the plastic bag of pellet food he kept there, solely to keep his feathered friends happy. He found the bag and was pleased that he did not have to drive across town to Baker's Feed Store. Curiosity about the contents of the letter gnawed at him as he pulled into the entrance of Kowalski Park, named for the man who had bequeathed to the city of Oak Grove land that was once a dairy. He drove slowly, keeping to the ten-mile-per-hour speed limit signs, past the white-painted bandstand with the pergola roof. On special holidays the bandstand was the scene of social activities such as German beer fests and Polish polka festivals. Things were quiet now at the bandstand, with only a young mother pushing a baby stroller, and a man walking his dog. Father Josiah always enjoyed the park most at this morning hour. It was early May and the clear blue skies promised another beautiful spring day. Continuing around the circular drive to the far end of the lake, away from the noise of the playground, he walked to the picnic bench closest to the water. After throwing a few handfuls of pellets to the visiting mallards and the resident white ducks, he took the long blue envelope out of his pocket. Removing the letter, he could not help but smile at seeing the familiar handwriting: "Dear Father Josiah."

Since his arrival at St. Andrews Russian Orthodox Church in Oak Grove, Kansas, just over three years ago, he had grown used to the precise language and formality of the countless lengthy notes from Helena. Many times, the notes were her own analysis of a point of Orthodox doctrine; at other times, the notes recounted an event in her life and the spiritual meaning it now contained. Most often though, they were simply letters concerning things she felt she could not or would not discuss openly during his meetings with her and her husband of almost sixty years. Married in 1943, they had shared many experiences together, but in spiritual matters, they differed considerably.

Helena had been an agnostic for many years following their emigration to the United States in the early 1950s. Her faith in God had been shaken by the senseless events surrounding the cruelty of war. Gennady, on the other hand, maintained an unquestioning faith. He simply accepted what was written and found comfort in the teachings of the church. He understood his wife and did not try to force things upon her, knowing she would resist all the more. Helena never interfered with Gennady's devotion to the Russian Orthodox faith, much less challenged him; nor did she seem to mind the countless hours he spent volunteering his efforts to help when called upon. But, try as she might, she simply could not lose her anger toward a God that allowed so many heartaches to occur. She used the time he spent away from home to pursue her own interests, such as gardening and cleaning. A change had been taking place over the last few years however and Helena found herself increasingly responsive to the desire within most people for spiritual knowledge. She began to read the Bible with regularity, searching for the truths that lay between the pages.

Father Mathias, the previous priest at St. Andrews, had been frail and sickly when Helena began her quest for understanding, leaving Helena to draw many of her own conclusions. With the arrival of the young and congenial Father Josiah, Helena pursued her religious studies with renewed interest. She had found him a brilliant scholar with a quick mind, along with a patient personality. Patience was certainly needed to deal with Helena's never-ending questions and her challenges to the often mystical side of Orthodoxy.

As a newly ordained priest, this gaunt young man, with the passion of his first church assignment, began to meet weekly with the elderly Russian couple. His deep-set dark eyes would sparkle with excitement when he sensed an understanding of the faith he had embraced as his calling. Born into a Presbyterian family, the former Thomas Burkett felt a growing emptiness following the sudden automobile deaths of both his mother and his father. His parents had converted to his newfound Orthodox faith shortly before their deaths—and he was grateful for that—but he sorely missed their presence in his life. After initially meeting the new priest who had replaced old Father Matthias, Gennady and Helena sensed in Josiah a man in need of a family and had embraced him warmly. In return, Father Josiah grew to love them both as he slowly became a part of their lives. The little house on Elm Place had become almost a second home for the young man in the early days of his first church assignment.

Over the past three years, as the church grew and his schedule became busier with the growing congregation, he barely had time for the weekly meetings with them. However, he always looked forward to Wednesdays and the spirited discussions with the ninety-year-old Gennady and his seventy-six-year-old wife. Their tiny living room, which became unbearably hot during the summer, drew them either to the covered patio or to the enclosed back porch.

The patio was the young priest's favorite place. Like the back porch, it was decorated in the pink, green, and white colors that were Helena's favorites. The wicker furniture was cozy on the porch, but the rose garden and chirping of the birds, gathered at one of the many feeders in the yard, was what Father Josiah enjoyed most. Most Wednesday mornings, the three people would be found sipping black tea and nibbling on poppy seed cakes while discussing Helena's ongoing church lessons. Imposing and dignified, as if holding court with his subjects, white-haired Gennady usually sat to the side, in a high-backed lounge chair, simply nodding his head from time to time, neither agreeing nor disagreeing with them. Helena usually sat on the wrought iron garden bench, with a stack of papers and books at her side for references. Josiah could always tell when Helena was pondering something that he had said by the way her hand would trace the flower design in the wrought iron of the bench before she answered. From time to time, she would reach through the side of the bench and touch her husband's knee if he began to doze. Gennady's unquestioning nature made it easier for Father Josiah to maintain a point with Helena, since he only had one of them to contend with. The one subject that Gennady did draw the line with though, was any discussion regarding the tsar.

As the spiritual head of the Orthodoxy, the murdered Tsar Nicholas had been looked upon as the leader of the faith. With his execution in 1918, it was felt that the spiritual heart of Russia had been murdered along with Nicholas and his family. Gennady held the memories of the martyr close. He entered the cadet academy as a child of twelve. It was while in cadet school that he heard of the assassination, leaving him bewildered and angry. He later fought bravely against the Red Army. When Lenin died in 1924, Gennady had just turned eighteen years old. Then came the brutality of Josef Stalin, which lasted twenty-four years.

The couple watched and saw the loss of life and property mount with increasing regularity, compounded by the invasion of Hitler's army. Gennady met Helena within that time period, but they were not to be married for ten more years when Gennady was almost thirty-five years old. In 1953, when emigration was possible, they made the trip to the United States through Norway, where they had escaped to safety after Germany's invasion of Poland. In total, between the two of them, they had lost four countries. Helena, from Yugoslavia, had escaped to Poland, then to Estonia and with the end of the war was summarily ordered to leave Norway. Gennady had taken a similar path.

Born and raised in the northern reaches of the vast Soviet Empire, as a child he witnessed the execution of his father and then suffered the loss of his mother and two sisters in a cholera epidemic that swept the countryside. An uncle took him to White Russia, now known as Belarus; and with some contacts and favors owed to him, they had placed him in a cadet school, where he fought bravely against the Red Army of Stalin. Marked for assassination by a false accusation, Gennady fled to neighboring Poland, where he met the intense dark eyes of his beloved Helena.

Father Josiah turned his attention back to the letter and continued reading Helena's precise handwriting:

Please accept our apology for the late timing of this note. Gennady and I have taken an earlier flight to Chicago so he can rest a bit before his next television interview tonight. Air travel seems to tire him out considerably and with the new medication, it is even more of a problem than usual. We will return on Tuesday and I will telephone to arrange our next meeting with you. Until then, Gennady and I will hold you in our thoughts and prayers.

Helena Gordovna Kiranovich

Father Josiah folded the letter and placed it back into the long, blue envelope. He sat for a moment, then bowed his head and prayerfully asked for God's protective love to surround these two amazing people. He would miss their presence at services this coming Sunday, but understood their reasons for not being there.

The success of Gennady's book astounded the elderly Russian couple, but had not changed their personalities or the way they looked at life. Gennady and Helena were traveling extensively lately, attending book signings as well as making television appearances to discuss their life prior to 1953.

At the beginning of the Cold War, Nikita Khrushchev was in power. The Communists made life intolerable for Russian citizens who remained in their homeland, while many who left, such as Helena and Gennady, with family who might still be alive, were afraid to speak out. Many former subjects under the tsar, even longed for a return to the old days, in bondage, but before the indiscriminate killing.

Finally, after so many years, they felt free and secure enough to tell their story. Helena, who seldom smiled and laughed even less, felt ill at ease with the attention; and Father Josiah knew she was always anxious to get back home, the only place she really felt safe. Gennady, having learned long ago to obey orders while in the military, placidly acquiesced to every demand by the publishers and Father Josiah had become increasingly concerned.

The bond between the couple was strong and unspoken words were filled with respect and love. Although Gennady was an undemonstrative man, he secretly admired Helena's courage and, as his years advanced and his health began to deteriorate, he relied on her strength more and more. It was Helena who remembered the exact timing of his medications and reminded him to eat *before* taking the yellow heart medication tablets and to take the white ones only *after* eating. It was she who discovered that three other medications prescribed for him counteracted each other and caused dizzying side effects. The insulin injections for his diabetes were also administered by Helena, as well as the daily pin-pricks in his finger that monitored his blood sugar. She kept a close eye on his diet as well, and cooked tasty food despite the seriousness of both his heart condition and the diabetes, both of which had taken its toll.

They had married in 1943 during another period of chaos in Russia. Together, they had survived Stalin and Hitler's onslaughts and together they had escaped through Nazi-occupied Poland—walking for days through a forest, dodging convoys of tanks until they found the American forces and managed to make themselves understood well enough to be taken to safety in Norway.

Father Josiah once asked them how they came to settle in Kansas, in the middle of a country they knew nothing about. Gennady explained how an immigration official asked if they had a preference where to resettle in America. Neither of them had any idea how to answer and looking around, they spotted some young soldiers.

Asking a young American soldier who spoke Russian where he was from, they listened intently. Using an old map of the United States, the soldier began to describe Kansas. They were drawn to his description of the flat landscape with flowing fields of wheat and corn. It reminded them of the rich fields of the Russian steppes. Together, the couple had chosen Kansas as a destination for their new lives. They worked hard and saved every penny they could, and, when they were able, they purchased the little house on Elm Place. In that tiny home, they raised their two children and established themselves among the community.

For some reason, whenever Father Josiah asked about their children, Victoria and Stephan, he was always met with stony silence and the subject was quickly changed. He never brought it up again, realizing that it was a touchy subject. Their children achieved success in their own right, with daughter Victoria becoming an aggressive criminal attorney in New York's borough of Brooklyn. Neither of the children had married, much to their parent's disappointment.

Large families were the mainstay of cultural survival, and although their son Stephan had fathered a child when he was in his twenties, he had refused to marry the girl. Instead, he left Oak Grove, abandoning his parents to face the accusing stares and uplifted eyebrows of their neighbors and friends. Not owning up to the responsibility was against everything his parents stood for and Stephan remained in self-imposed exile up until the present. Rarely returning to his childhood home, he had chosen a military career and lived a nomadic life, mostly in foreign posts that he requested. Gennady and Helena knew very little of the child he had fathered. In confidence, Helena had told Josiah, they found out later, it was a dark-eyed boy named John. Again, she had dropped the subject abruptly after their discussion. He remained a mystery to his biological father, as well as to his grandparents and no one seemed to know if he was still in the area or if his mother had taken him away permanently when she left town in disgrace.

All that was known was her first name and an old photograph Helena found after Stephan left home. It was a high school dance photo with an unsmiling Stephan standing next to a stunning young girl in a green prom dress. As far as Helena knew, this was the only social event her handsome son attended with a girl throughout his high school days. She presumed it must be the only girl that Stephan had developed an interest in, and deduced that this must be the mother of their only grandchild. All Helena knew about her was her name, scribbled on the back of the picture: Eilie. Gennady never questioned why his wife had placed the picture in a small silver frame on the bookshelf. Gradually, over the years, it had been pushed back into the shadows and Father Josiah never noticed it.

Occasionally a postcard would arrive, the only contact Helena had with her son and they never had a return address. The mere mention of Stephan's name would set Gennady's jaw into a tight line and Father Josiah had learned not to bring up the subject of his children with him.

Their daughter, Victoria, was equally estranged from her parents. From an old high school photograph, Father Josiah could see that she had grown into a large figure of a woman, resembling her barrel-chested, tall father and not her diminutive mother. Denying this rather masculine appearance, Helena had insisted on attempting to feminize her daughter as she grew up, selecting unbecoming lacy pink dresses and placing large bows in her stringy hair. The humiliation by her very "Americanized" peers, affected the girl. It didn't help that she also developed acne and her mother refused to let her use anything but caustic yellow laundry soap on it, avoiding new "cosmetic" medications.

More and more Victoria withdrew, becoming sullen and angry as she passed from childhood into womanhood. A sense of failing to please her mother was ever-present. Although Victoria was a brilliant student, her desire to achieve and to prove her own worth hid beneath the open hostility toward her traditions and culture. Victoria refused to attend Russian celebrations and often had the audacity to openly criticize the late Tsar Nicholas and his family, causing her father to explode in anger and send her to her room. Victoria left home after graduating from high school and never looked back. Hitching a ride to the East Coast, she was soon swallowed up in the mass of people there who were only concerned with their own survival and oblivious to her plight. Small temporary jobs were all she could find in the beginning and her odd appearance became even more of a detriment during interviews. Job searching proved fruitless, but after months wandering on the streets of New York, she had found solace. If not for the concern of a woman who ran a soup kitchen, it is likely that Victoria would have traveled a much different road in life.

The soup kitchen volunteer, Anna Stein, had taken the homely young girl under her wing and helped her to recognize her talents. Anna knew how being different could destroy, having felt like a misfit since her arrival from a predominantly Jewish enclave to an Irish Catholic neighborhood. Volunteering her time at the soup kitchen helped Anna to satisfy her desire to help others, no matter who they were. She befriended all who needed help and easily became accepted by the disenfranchised in the street community. Anna was herself a huge woman, towering over most men, and with a bawdy sense of humor that she used liberally. She was the first person to point out her huge feet and hands, and her sausage-shaped index finger would point to the unsightly birthmark on her forehead. Rather disconcerting, the irregular-shaped strawberry blemish appeared to creep just under her hairline and continued across the top of her eyebrow. It was remarkable in that, from a certain angle, it had the shape of the profile of the Roman Catholic Pope. Anna would laugh in her hearty way and say, "I am a Jewess, but I carry a picture of the Pope for added insurance."

With Anna's encouragement, Victoria applied for an education grant. With her academic scores from Oak Grove High School, she was not only given the grant, but after her first year of study won a scholarship as well. Victoria attended law school and graduated with honors, without her parent's presence or their knowledge. The acne-scarred round face of the daughter of immigrants had her diploma in hand as she hugged the elderly Jewish woman who had given her the love and support that her critical mother found difficult to give. It was Anna who Victoria turned to when she had a problem, and Anna who was privy to the hopes and dreams of the girl who never had a date or a boyfriend. However, like dutiful daughters all over the world, Victoria sent Christmas and Mother's Day cards to Helena, who never realized she had lost her daughter's love to another woman who accepted her unconditionally. How surprised she would have been to learn that Anna Stein's niece was wearing the pink, lace-trimmed sweaters that she still sent to Victoria each Christmas.

Father Josiah again looked at his watch and was surprised to see that two hours had passed so quickly. The sun was high overhead as he left the lake to the ducks and drove quickly to his next parish home visit. It was almost dinnertime when he finished his homebound calls for the day.

Waiting for him at his office in St. Andrews was the blinking red light on the cheap answering machine. Absently pressing the *Play* button, he was surprised to hear Helena's distraught voice sobbing on the tape. She was almost incoherent and he pushed *Replay* to listen again. With numbing shock, he heard that Gennady was dead. He had taken a nap in the hotel room and Helena could not rouse him to get ready for the television taping that evening. In deep distress, in between sobs, Father Josiah learned that the flight bringing her home would be arriving in the morning and that the body of her husband would be flown out the next day. Helena requested the services to held as soon as possible and at the very end of the message, she pleaded, "Please be there to meet my flight, Father." He replayed the message three times to be sure he had not misunderstood and wrote the flight information down on the little pink pad twice. In a stunned voice, young Josiah said, "Of course I will be there," aloud to the machine. Automatically, he began to pray.

Half an hour later, he made a few hasty phone calls to prepare for the service for a man who had lived such a courageous life, then Father Josiah placed his head on his arms and wept bitter tears for this person whom he had become so fond of.

Helena arrived on American Airlines, flight 612, her eyes swollen from crying, but impeccably attired in a navy blue unwrinkled suit and crisp white blouse. She hugged Father Josiah and together they left the airport in his old yellow Datsun, driving to the little white house on Elm Place. Arrangements were made with Peter Yelkov at Oak Grove Mortuary to take care of Gennady when he arrived. Out of habit, Father

Josiah and Helena went out to the back patio and took their usual seats. Longingly, Helena glanced at the empty high-backed chair where Gennady used to sit; but then, with pursed lips, she forced herself to go over in minute detail the order of service to be held on Friday.

Father Josiah gently asked, "Is there anyone you would like me to notify for you, Babushka?"

There was a long pause as Helena traced the sides of the wrought iron bench before she spoke. "I would like our children to be told first," she said. Then her face took on a lost look as she added, "But I am not sure how to reach them."

Father Josiah held the hands of the old woman and softly said, "Please don't worry, we'll find them."

Assuring him that she would be fine if he left, Helena rose wearily and saw him to the door. Before he left, she gave him the last known address she had for Victoria, where she had sent last year's sweater. Father Josiah drove off, leaving her with her grief. As he drove back to St. Andrews, he wondered if he would find Victoria and Stephan with the slim bits of information Helena had given him.

Victoria was easy to find after all. With only two phone calls, he found himself speaking to the daughter of his dear friends for the first time. He was surprised that she took the news of her father's death with so little emotion. She briskly told him that she would "check the calendar" and "if possible" would attend the funeral. The priest quickly asked if she had any idea how to reach her brother. She placed him on hold for ten minutes, returning with the information that she had no idea and had not been in touch with him for years. The conversation ended with the address of the funeral home so she could "send flowers, at least."

Father Josiah was saddened by the complete lack of interest and wished he knew what had caused the deep rips in the fabric of the lives of this family. To do that, he would have to know what had caused the rips to begin with and he knew that would be difficult. The next two hours would be spent attempting to reach Stephan. Finally, with the help of the military locator and Stephan's social security number from Helena, he was found.

"So, the old man is gone, eh?" said Stephan bitterly.

Father Josiah cringed at the hostility in the deep voice on the other end. "Your father was a devout man of the Orthodox faith," he assured Stephan.

"Right and I suppose you didn't notice the shrine to the tsar in the corner? Idolizing him was the last thing I ever wanted to do."

"That's a bit complicated, but not uncommon for those who saw the tsar as the embodiment of the faith," Josiah explained. "It doesn't follow that he is worshipped, however, merely that he is respected and honored."

"Well, whatever, it's part of the 'old country' and all I ever heard about from the old man," he answered defiantly. I don't think he ever understood that he wasn't in the 'old country' anymore."

Father Josiah felt the blood rising in his face and prayed for patience. He searched for the right words and finally said, "The 'old country' as you call it, taught your father the principles of decency and compassion. When he saw that taken over by lies and deceit, it grieved him deeply. Yes, he had an attachment, an attachment that he tried to pass on to you and to your sister. Perhaps if you had really listened to the message behind his words, you would have realized this. Your absence from his life also grieved him deeply. I only hope you will come and say goodbye to him now."

Stephan laughed. "You don't have any idea what you are talking about, Father. You didn't have to live with his strict codes of morality." He added, "I won't make any promises." Then, his voice softened and he quietly asked, "How is my mother?"

Father Josiah spent the next half-hour speaking calmly to the gruff man in an attempt to tell him of his parents. He tried to persuade him that his father was an honorable man who gave much of his time to the church and its programs. He told him about the many emigrants who Gennady had helped to adjust in Oak Grove and of his mother's feelings of loss and grief now that she was alone. By the end of the conversation, Stephan agreed to "try" to attend the funeral and promised to make arrangements to be in Oak Grove. Father Josiah offered to pick him up at the airport, but Stephan declined.

The conversation ended and the young priest stared sadly at the phone. He wondered how he would give Helena the comfort she needed to cope with her loss without the support of her children. He did not expect Victoria to pay her last respects, but hoped she would have second thoughts and her love for her mother would prevail over her "busy schedule." She did promise to call back and leave a message if she made travel plans later that day, so he tried to be optimistic.

Father Josiah suddenly remembered he had to call the president of the Parish Women's Group. Olga Levchenkov was in charge of the women who would prepare the *Zakuski* for after the services. These traditional foods; marinated mushrooms, salted herring, smoked salmon, cold tongue, and red beet salad—were prepared for all who attended and would need time to assemble. He called, leaving a message for Olga on her machine.

Although Helena did not have many close friends in the church, he knew they would respond to her during this time of need with compassion as they always did. He then called Victor, the head of the Men's Parish Group, to arrange for special prayers and asked for the protocol at the cemetery for such an honorable man. Once again, he was met with an answering machine and left a message.

Confident that all would be taken care of, Father Josiah checked his watch. His father had given him that watch when he left for the seminary. He gratefully recalled that his father had always been supportive of his ideas and efforts when he was alive. It was difficult for the young priest to reconcile a father and son being estranged for any reason. He knew there must be a cause for Stephan's hostility toward his father, beyond the reasons of ideology. Father Josiah walked through the door of his office that connected with the interior of the church.

He stood, silently focused on the icon of St. John the Wonder Worker, struggling to bring the countless visits and conversations with Helena and Gennady into his thoughts. His lips moving in silent prayer, he asked for answers to the mystery of the pain in this fragmented family. One thing he did know for certain was that without forgiveness there could be no healing. He recited the ancient prayer of the heart, *Lord Jesus Christ, Son of God, have mercy on me and forgive me my sins.* Over and over, he repeated the prayer as he counted each knot on his prayer rope. In his studies at the seminary, Father Josiah learned about the mystic world of deep prayers and about visions that others had seen. This had never been his priority—he was simply seeking a path towards reconciliation.

Josiah stood, repeating over and over the simple prayer until it penetrated his mind, his heart and his whole being. The Prayer of the Heart was always silently running, much like a computer program ran, in the background of his mind. Now, he brought it to the forefront and consciously poured out his concern with each word. With every breath, he prayed to be a good priest and feeling his own unworthiness, he asked for forgiveness. In so doing, he opened his heart to connection with the Divine, as he asked for assistance. A feeling of ecstasy filled his being as he entered an almost altered state of consciousness. Almost immediately, he found himself transported to a summer afternoon. The bees buzzed around the roses in their perfectly pruned bed. The pinks and greens of the plastic table-cover flowers came into sight. He vividly saw the garden bench with the grape arbor behind it. Helena came into the vision, absently tracing the design of the bench with her finger. Picking up the conversation with her, he could hear the soft snoring of Gennady in the background, sitting in the high-backed chair as usual.

Helena lowered her voice to a whisper, but Father Josiah could clearly hear her words: "He will never forgive him and I can't understand the church teaching on forgiving. I thought that forgiveness was a part of love. How can you explain why someone cannot forgive?" Then, in an almost inaudible whisper, as if talking to herself, she added, "Even his own son." This was many years ago and Father Josiah shook his head and shrugged his shoulders. When Helena realized he did not have an easy answer, she continued, "Then I think I will have to continue to ask God and never stop asking for this forgiveness to take place." He had been a priest for such a short time back then and had not heard their story completely. The conversation had never come up again.

The scene changed rapidly and this time Father Josiah was leaving the little house through the front door. As he was shown the fast-moving images, one item on the crowded bookshelves came sharply into focus. It was a small silver frame with a photo of a young man with heavy eyebrows standing stiffly next to a striking young woman. The image dissolved as a voice broke Father Josiah's concentration.

"Father Josiah, excuse me please," a man's voice said. The voice came from Alex Petrevic, from the Men's Parish Committee. He explained that he was checking on the time for the services for Gennady on Friday. The two men returned to Father Josiah's office where they made the final arrangements for the order of the service. The remainder of the afternoon was taken up with routine business, and as evening drew to a close, the young priest decided to stop by Helena's home after his evening meal to check on her.

As he was parking the Datsun, he saw Mrs. Kelly racing towards him.

"Father, please, come right away. Helena is at my house and she seems in a daze. I tried to get her to talk, but she refuses to speak English and I don't know what she is saying. I tried to call you, but you already had left your office. Thank God you came here, I don't know what to do!"

Josiah jumped quickly out of his car and dashed to the open door of Mrs. Kelly's home. Inside he found a disheveled Helena sitting on the green sofa, rocking back and forth, tears running down her pale cheeks. Her silky white hair was undone and she was speaking incoherently in Russian. The priest knelt down in front of her, taking her hands in his. Seeing the vacant look in her eyes, he softly said, "Helena, Helena, you are not alone—God is with you, I am with you, and Gennady will always be in your heart. Please talk to me in English, Helena." There was no response from the old woman, who continued babbling.

Mrs. Kelly, standing off to the side, quietly said, "I was looking out of my front window and saw her walking in the front yard. She was stepping all over the hyacinths. I knew there must be something wrong because she spent so much time on her flower beds. She was stomping on them and cutting the roses down with her shears. I went over to her, but all she did was cry and speak in Russian. I didn't know what to do, so I brought her home. She seemed to calm down and then suddenly she looked around the room and went out of control again. I don't know what happened, but every time I asked where her husband was, she just sobbed and sobbed. I'm so glad now that you're here to help her. I know she thinks the world of you, Father."

With that, Mrs. Kelly looked beseechingly at Josiah. The priest told her about Gennady's death and the woman immediately made the sign of the cross on herself and asked God's blessing for his soul. Father Josiah looked around the room at the numerous statues of the Virgin Mary and smiled to himself. "The faith of a true believer never goes unnoticed by God," he thought. He glanced again around the room and his eyes opened with amazement. On the mantel above the red brick fireplace was a small white ceramic picture frame with a shamrock painted on the edge. It was the photo in the vision! The only difference was the frame. The green shamrock enhanced the emerald green of the dress worn by a young woman with green eyes and long auburn hair. It was a stark contrast to the unsmiling face of the young man next to her with a brooding look under heavy eyebrows.

The vision he experienced standing in front of the icons a short time ago immediately flashed into his mind, but he could not decipher the meaning. What did all of this mean? The word *forgiveness* also came into his thoughts. "How?" he muttered. Did this have anything to do with the forgiveness Helena had spoken of in the vision? Confused, Father Josiah decided to attend to the needs of Helena first. He asked Mrs. Kelly if he could use her phone and called Olga at home, asking her to meet him at Helena's house. Gently, he took Helena by the arm to lead her back to her own home. He thanked Mrs. Kelly and asked if he could come back and talk with her. She assured him that her door was always open to him and that the tea kettle would be on.

Olga arrived within minutes and took Helena into the bedroom. Father Josiah went in afterwards, and both he and Olga recited the traditional evening prayer:

> Lord our God, as Thou art good and the Lover of mankind, forgive me wherein I have sinned today in word, deed and thought. Grant me peaceful and undisturbed sleep: send Thy guardian angel to protect and keep me from evil. For Thou art the Guardian of our souls and bodies, and unto Thee do we send up glory to the Father and to the Son, and to the Holy Spirit, now and forever, and unto the ages of ages. Amen.

Olga promised to stay until Helena was asleep and began to talk softly to her in Russian, which seemed to calm Helena down and she drifted off to sleep. Just as Father Josiah began to leave, Olga beckoned for him to wait.

Joining him in the living room, she said, "Father, Helena keeps mumbling something about her grandson; but I didn't think Helena and Gennady had a grandson. Do you know anything about this?"

"No," answered Josiah, "but I'm going to try and find out."

It was dark outside and as Olga opened the front door for him, he turned to say goodbye. The street lamp in front of the house cast a shaft of light that caught his eye. A small silver frame was glinting in the light; Father Josiah caught his breath sharply. He went straight to the frame, but could not believe his eyes. It was the same scowling face of the young man and his smiling red-haired friend in the green dress! Without a word to the startled Olga, he grabbed the frame and headed out the door. Running across the street, and up the porch steps, he frantically knocked on Mrs. Kelly's door. She opened it to find a breathless Josiah holding a picture frame in his hands.

"Father, is everything all right with Helena?"

"Please," began the priest, "tell me who is in this photograph."

"Why, that's Eilie," said Mrs. Kelly, her eyes open wide. "How did you get a picture of her?"

"Eilie? Eilie? Who is Eilie?"

"Eilie, short for Eileen, is my niece. Please, Father let me make some tea. I think we need to talk."

For the next two hours, Mrs. Kelly told Father Josiah about the girl in the emerald green dress. She told him that the picture was from the Senior Prom, but she didn't know the boy in the picture. She told him of a child, born out of wedlock to her and how it had been kept by the girl, despite the shame of it for an Irish Catholic family. She told Father Josiah that her niece had been sent to live with her in Pennsylvania and later moved back to Kansas. The girl never married and she and her son now lived in a suburb of Kansas City. She had the phone number and address in her little book.

Suddenly, it all began to make sense to Josiah as the story unfolded. He told Mrs. Kelly that the boy standing next to her niece was Stephan, the son of her Russian neighbor. Helena had the same picture on the crowded bookshelf toward the back and he had never noticed it until tonight.

Mrs. Kelly kept shaking her head, saying, "This can't be possible." She got up and returned with a photo album. On one of the pages, there was a recent picture of a teenage boy wearing a Scout uniform. A serious, unsmiling face with heavy eyebrows looked back at them as Mrs. Kelly slowly said, "That is Eileen's son—his name is John." There was no mistaking the resemblance.

There was silence at the table. Mrs. Kelly spoke first, "Father, what shall we do now?"

"I wish I knew, I wish I knew," he answered, shaking his head. "Whatever we do must be in the best interests of all, but that's the only thing I'm sure of at this moment." The two people sat staring speechlessly at the photos of the young girl and the stern face of the young man. The smaller photo of the graduate was propped between them and there could be no mistake. In different frames, but duplicate images, the pictures held the answers to many questions. Neither of them said a word, both lost in their own thoughts. Finally, Father Josiah reached out to take Helena's silver frame. He asked with his eyes if he could also take the graduation photo and Mrs. Kelly nodded.

Quietly, Father Josiah left the Kelly home and walked across the street to the little house with the pink shutters and broken flowers. Stopping before he got to the door, he looked at the house for a moment and then turned away from it. He walked quickly to his old Datsun and laid the photos on the seat next to him before driving back to St. Andrews.

The little red light was blinking again on the answering machine in his office. Father Josiah placed the frame and photo on his desk and pushed the *Play* button. A deep voice with an abrupt tone said, "This is Captain Kiranovich. I am calling to give you my flight information and would appreciate a meeting with you at the airport upon my arrival." He went on to give the pertinent details, which Father Josiah wrote on his memo pad. The machine rewound automatically and Josiah realized there had been no message from Victoria.

The hour was late and although Father Josiah was exhausted, he knew he had to go into the church before he tried to sleep. Entering the nave of the church, he walked toward the iconostasis. The beautiful wooden partition that concealed the altar from view held many of the icon images of saints that connect the blessings of God to the faithful. It was time for the midnight prayer and as he began the ritual, his eyes focused on his favorite icon.

The image of St. John the Wonder Worker gazed back at him as his fingers moved automatically along the knots of his prayer cord. Father Josiah began to think of the life of the zealous missionary leader of the Russian Orthodox faith. St. John was not only a brilliant theologian, but a great Holy Elder in the mystic traditions of the faith. It was said that he could hear thoughts and answer them before they were expressed. Since his death in 1966, many miracles had been attributed to his intercessions. Father Josiah was often drawn to him and in this particular case, where it concerned a child, it seemed most appropriate. St. John had done much for the benefit of children. He had organized homes for orphans and children of the needy in many parts of the world. Deep in thought, Father Josiah placed the face in the graduation photo in his mind as he began to pray. It took only moments for the young priest to feel the presence of love surrounding him. All alone, in the darkened church, he silently asked guidance to meet the coming days and prayed for Gennady's soul.

Suddenly, Josiah found himself immersed in a sea of blue light. The blue immediately gave way to white and a figure seemed to be was walking toward him. Wearing his black Sunday suit, adorned with all of his colorful medals and sash, he was grinning broadly. Josiah was startled to be looking at the face of his old friend, Gennady. Much to his surprise, however, Gennady walked right past him, his shoulder brushing the priest's arm as he passed. Father Josiah turned slightly and saw the old man, walking now without effort, clasp the shoulders of a tall man and kiss him on both cheeks. Josiah drew his breath in sharply and saw that it was Stephan. The image disappeared and Father Josiah was once again standing alone in the dark church, his prayer cord in his hand. A feeling of peace came over him and he silently gave thanks with a comforting feeling that everything would now reach its proper conclusion.

* * *

When Father Josiah met with Captain Kiranovich the next day, a peculiar conversation took place. The military man began to tell him of a strange dream the night before.

"In this dream, I felt as though my father had truly forgiven me and I think it's time now to return to Oak Grove and make up for the time I've lost with my mother," he said. Josiah felt it was the right moment to tell Stephan about his son.

Helena quickly recovered from her grief with the same strength that had carried her through all of life's ordeals. She was comforted by the sudden appearance of her daughter, Victoria, who entered the church in time to kiss her father goodbye. Victoria, a self-sufficient and successful woman, now practices law in Kansas and visits frequently. Eileen and Stephan are good friends and both are involved with John's life. Gennady's words are often used by everyone: "Papa used to say..."

"It's never too late to forgive."

Kristina

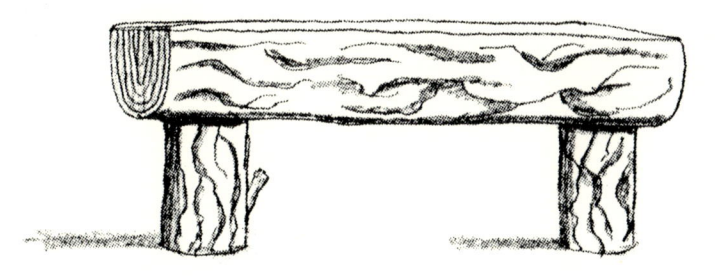

L ike sap exploding in the yellow flames of a fire, the sound rang out, sharp and clear, disturbing the silence of the forest. Kristina's weathered axe once again bit into the log at her feet. Three more times she lifted the heavy tool to the shoulders of her short, stocky frame. With practiced rhythm, it was guided into the wood with a force that only gravity and her sixty-two-year-old arms could combine. At last, on the fifth attempt, the log surrendered into two, almost equal, pieces. The chill in the air foretold the start of another relentless Siberian winter. In a few weeks, the earth would begin its freeze-thaw cycle and the same log would surrender again. This time, it would be to the iron stove at the heart of Kristina's one-room log home. She repeated the chore with gravity, arms and willpower reducing two more pieces of dead tree to manageable size. Awake since 4:00 A.M., it was now shortly after dawn on a Friday in late September. Kristina lifted the hem of her skirt and knelt on the frosted grass. Thinning white hair escaped a floral cotton scarf firmly knotted beneath her chin. The hair underneath, unbraided, fell loosely to her shoulders, framing the high cheekbones of a face that seemed far too aged for its deep-set blue eyes. For a moment, she rested on her knees with her left hand supporting her, trying to recapture breath stolen by age and the morning chores.

The woodcutting ended as it did yesterday, and the day before, and the day before that. The same routine had been unchanged for as long as she could remember. Of course Kristina's memory was not what it once was, nor was her hearing. Otherwise, a life of labor as a peasant had conditioned both her mind and body for the solitary life she led.

To her left sat an oval willow basket, dark brown and very long–its handle of tightly braided reeds arched gracefully over nearly vertical sides. When she carried it, the basket dangled about mid-calf and only a foot off the ground. Using a well-practiced move, Kristina raked the fingers of her cupped hand through the grass, gathering the smaller debris of the chopping and placing it in the basket to be used for kindling. Out of habit and necessity, nothing in Kristina's life was wasted.

Before stepping inside the doorway of her home, she sniffed the air. Noting there was no moisture present, she smiled. She knew the day would remain dry and therefore, no need to wear her heavy boots for the monthly trip to the village. The soles of her father's boots had worn through again and she reminded herself to replace the worn rabbit skins inside for cushioning when she returned. Placing the basketful of tiny wood chips on the table, she retrieved three small logs from the woodpile and stacked them next to the stove, ready to be used when she returned at dusk.

For breakfast, the old woman selected an apple from another basket on the table. It was a bit drier than she liked, but still pleasingly sweet. By the time juicier apples would again fill her handmade baskets, the thought of this last fruit of the season would be appealing. She took the apple to the only chair in her home, a small wooden rocker, facing the window. It was just an arm's length from the cooking stove, standing slightly off-center in the square room. The chimney flue of a small cast-iron stove skirted one of the hand-hewn timbers supporting the thatched roof. Because it took such effort to feed the hungry stove, she was frugal with its diet.

Kristina was frugal with her own diet as well. Usually, preparing soups cooked for hours over small fires and often choosing raw foods, rather than wasting fuel on cooking. Along the back wall stood her bed and a large, rustic pine chest containing a sparse wardrobe. Kristina's most valued possessions were kept in an ornate wooden box that held a small lacquered brooch from her late mother and a jeweled icon. Kristina never displayed the icon, possibly because she didn't think to do so. Her late father hid it in the wooden box from authorities when their religion of Eastern Orthodoxy was outlawed and it was not part of her daily routine, she had too many other things that seemed more important than worship.

The window, the only one in the house, distinguished the east wall. Four lead glass panes looked in above a kitchen counter and a basin where a hand pump stood ready. The small window gave a view to the horizon. Looking out at the black line of the forest, preceded by a gently descending meadow, her eyes quickly scanned her prized garden. Just a month ago, instead of woodcutting, she spent her mornings harvesting the vegetables and herbs that would feed her through the winter when wind and cold kept her housebound. Burlap sacks and baskets of potatoes, turnips, beets, carrots, squash and onions now filled the dirt cellar dug along the east wall foundation. Opposite the single window was the west wall, where a long shelf hung above a well-worn plank table.

Kristina's attention, now that her parents were deceased, was centered on a cat called Kutzya. From a respectable distance, he watched her finish the apple. Not that he would ever touch it! Mice, grasshoppers and moths were his mainstay. He fed himself, and performed a useful purpose, thereby making him an ideal pet for practical Kristina. Rising from the rocker, she smiled and teased the large tabby, calling him "Kitska," a term of endearment. The tattered wool blanket that padded the chair and slatted wooden backrest of the rocker invited the old cat to jump into the warmth left behind by Kristina's body. It was impossible to make out the pattern of the blanket, other than shades of faded red and white, but that was of no concern to either the cat or to Kristina. For each of them, it served its purpose.

She began to prepare her things for her trip to the village. Once again, it was market day. The village market used to be a thirty-minute stroll to a waiting line of hours for some hard crusted bread. Brought in by truck twice a week, the bread was a staple in everyone's diet. Kristina's gait was much slower now and the walk took a bit longer each month. Her steps were more cautious, but at least the wait in lines was much shorter.

Lines were a thing of the past, attributed to former President Mikhail Gorbachev's policy of *glasnost* or openness. Privatization had released merchants from state controls, freeing them to make and sell the same bread at whatever prices the market would pay. True, the lines were gone, but reform was bittersweet. Those like Kristina, beyond employment age and without extended family for support, could barely afford bread at the free-market prices. A couple of hours in line had been part of the price for the loaves baked, shipped and rationed by the central government. The price of *not* standing in a line was now more costly bread. The difference for Kristina was, now in the twilight of life, she was richer in the currency of time than in the currency of cash. If not for a tiny government pension, a love of gardening, the abundance of natural materials, and the craftsmanship to weave baskets, she would not survive.

Standing in line was also like the yeast in the recipe of the community. Friendships developed, and relationships rose and fell as the villagers inched toward the shops. Idle time, yes; idle talk, no. News of events and families, chores and church, successes and failures, as well as philosophy and politics, flowed freely through those lines.

Kristina reached for one of twenty baskets on the long shelf, the only semblance of decoration in her home. These beautiful finished baskets were for barter, however, and not for aesthetics. Kristina traded them for tools, garden seeds and other necessities in the village. On special occasions and near holidays, she exchanged them for chickens or a bit of meat. Similar baskets in various stages of completion were stacked in no particular fashion on the floor or any other level surface in the tiny house. The overall effect was a pleasant, cozy feeling, filled with the smells of various dried grasses and textured with shape and colors. The window glass, rain spotted and dirty on the outside and dusty on the inside from the basket debris, dulled the morning sun. The autumn sun was still bright enough for its rays to shed shades of gray and black shadows behind the white, tan and brown baskets. Along the timber and stone wall beneath the shelf, the gifts of nature—reeds, willows, bark, twigs, straw and wild grasses—wait for new form, new life, in Kristina's creative hands.

Electric power in this rural village was erratic. So it was by oil lantern and candles that Kristina formed her unique designs. Her rough, wrinkled hands were not merely dependable tools; they did the thinking as she carried on one-way conversations with Kitska about what *used* to be and what *is*. The baskets, each one hours in the making, ranged from utilitarian versions for gathering eggs and baskets made for the market, to elegant creations designed for decoration in the homes of the well-to-do visitors who occasionally came through the village. The latter included purse-like shapes with tightly woven covers, hinged with peeled bark and latched with gnarled twigs. They were her finest work, although she never thought of them as practical.

Kristina pulled the heavy door shut and then, remembering the cat, decided to leave it ajar. She squinted at the still-rising sun and began walking towards the center of town. The old woman double-checked the knot under her chin. Finding it secure, she pulled her blue flowered head-scarf extremely forward out of habit. Over her heavy gray sweater, she threw her shawl over her shoulders. The layers would help keep the morning chill at bay.

She did not travel the wild grass path more than once a month, certainly not enough to have worn a path, and the vegetation cushioned each step while slightly scenting the air. Soon the old woman arrived at the more traveled hard-packed dirt. Here was the road going east toward the cobblestone streets of the village. At this point though, the dirt road was more like a trail, just wide enough for a single horse-drawn cart. Kristina was not concerned about where the road might lead if she were to head further west on it. She turned westward only on religious holidays to attend church, and then just nine miles in that direction. There *was* a bus from the village, but bus fare would have been a luxury for this thrifty woman.

Heading towards the village, Kristina's flat-soled sturdy leather shoes picked up the brownish-gray dust of the road. The deposits settled into the creases and with a little imagination could have been a road map of Russia's burgeoning cities. Beyond the horizon lay the metropolis of St. Petersburg and the second-tier cities of Perm, Samara and Novnij. They were not alluring places for the elderly Kristina, and what she knew of them weighed heavily on her mind and heart. It was the growth of these cities that was tempting many of the village's young people away. Kristina sighed, knowing her friend, Zoya, who would be waiting for her at the crossroad today, was constantly talking about this subject. Kristina knew that seeking fast money and an even faster lifestyle most often returned trouble to the adventurous young people. Approaching the streets of the village, Kristina saw the familiar short form waving to her. She recognized the high raspy voice of Zoya calling to her, "Zdrasvootchi, hello, come sit, come sit and rest!" Patting the stone wall that encircled a small fountain, Zoya beckoned to her lifelong friend.

Somewhere in her sixties, but not one to reveal her exact age even to her best friend, Zoya smiled and embraced Kristina. The women sat close, one panting and the other waiting for her to catch her breath before they could begin talking. Zoya was almost bursting with gossip. An outspoken woman, she equally enjoyed both rumor and fact. This explained her habit for "overhearing" things while picking through fruit and vegetables in the outdoor market. *Almost* always though, Zoya was accurate in recounting stories. Moments after sitting down, as if on cue, a teen-aged girl briskly crossed the square in front of them.

"There," Zoya said, and nodded emphatically toward her, unashamed that the girl might notice she was this morning's hot topic. "Natalia, Natalia Petrenko. Barely fifteen years old and rumor has it that she is pregnant! Fifteen! They say she is leaving tomorrow for Novnij. Leaving her parents! Poor Igor and sickly Nadezhda. Leaving her parents so she can be with that, that *boyfriend*," she almost spat out the words.

Kristina was slow to respond to this news. She always articulated inwardly before speaking, even when Kutzya was the only one to hear her.

"So, she is pregnant," she said, unfazed. "She is no different from many of the young these days."

Zoya's husky voice reflected too many years of smoking cigarettes and continued to express disdain for Natalia and her *boyfriend*. With his pierced nose and strange haircut, he seemed to personify the changes that were creeping into the village, the result of influences from the new "Western" societies. "Who lived here in the old times would have thought about green hair color or rings in noses? It is unnatural!" railed Zoya.

But it was neither the girl's youth nor the out-of-wedlock pregnancy that caused her strong reaction. It was the girl's choice to leave the village that fueled Zoya's indignation. The teenage pregnancy was bad, but it could easily have been taken care of—too easily. It was not unthinkable for women of Natalia's generation to undergo a half-dozen abortions in their childbearing years, a tragic means of birth control in a country where contraceptives were expensive or unavailable.

In 1922, after the Bolshevik Revolution, Kristina knew that the Soviet Union had been the first nation to allow women to have abortions on demand; Stalin revoked that right in 1936, but it was restored again by Khrushchev in the 1950s. All of this Kristina had heard from Zoya many times before. No, it was not the pregnancy. What truly irritated Zoya was the girl's decision to move to Novnij.

"For years small villages like ours have been growing anemic," continued Zoya, "and now another drop of lifeblood, its youth, is spilled! Drop after drop leaves our village. It was only three months ago that Natalia's boyfriend and his circle of friends left here and bled the countryside, and now, the girl."

The old woman shook her head. Kristina couldn't understand how the grit, grime and crime of Novnij or any of dozens of other Russian cities was preferable to life in the quiet village for so many young adults.

"Don't they see that we are old, but that our lives are longer and richer from hard outside work?" Zoya continued. "A factory, instead of a farm—they think *that* can make them happy?"

Kristina didn't comment. She simply stood up, her very action inviting Zoya to join her, and hoped the tiresome conversation would end. They crossed the cobblestone plaza, while Zoya continued to lament the latest generation and the effects on their village. Kristina nodded from time to time, agreeing with her. Yes, Natalia was destined for a small flat in a drab block of crowded buildings. The future of the naive farm girl would be a menial, low-paying job, the kind that was filled with uneducated women. She would no doubt eventually wind up as a clerk or, if *very* lucky, working as a clerical helper in education or social services. Perhaps as a food worker or banking—if she was really lucky. Pulling the wagon behind her, Kristina listened with patience as Zoya once again told her the same story.

Zoya droned on and on about Russia having one of the world's highest percentages of females in the workplace; that nearly three in four working-age women were employed, accounting for forty-eight percent of all workers. Still, poor Natalia's prospects were not rosy despite an official policy of equal pay for equal work for men and women. Even with a government-mandated child care stipend for working mothers for the eighteen months after childbirth, Kristina heard that the earning power of the typical Russian woman was about forty percent of a male.

Natalia's boyfriend and his clique, all in their early twenties, were drawn to Novnij's textile mill by the lure of a monthly wage. Many times, however this wage was in the form of a few cases of vodka, or other goods, rather than in rubles.

"They live in a material world," Zoya continued, "as young people of their generation probably do everywhere nowadays. Do they really think that a paycheck—a piece of paper!—can buy character and fortitude? No, such things come from the labor of the farmers and herders who supply their mills, but this would never occur to these young people. No, they lack the patience to nurture a garden, grow and harvest a crop, or to husband sheep, goats and cattle! By day our young men work the cloth cutters and monitor the dye vats. By night, they drink, carouse and worse! Some of them even use drugs; and when they don't have enough money to buy them, what do they do? They turn to theft and violence!"

Talk of cities always made Kristina cringe. She wished that Zoya would change the subject, but allowed her to chatter away while her own mind tried not to recall the horrible incident six years ago. She shuddered whenever she thought of that awful day when she was robbed in Novnij, a victim of what the city does to decent young men. In the years since, she had not returned. The "City," *any* city, came to stand in her mind for all social ills.

Zoya finally came to a halt, "So, do you agree with me Kristina?"

Carefully answering, Kristina began to voice her thoughts. "Every person in a *village* is exposed to other people all the time. Then, they go to a city and they change. No one sees their lives and no one pays attention to them. They think they can live how they want and work how they want. In the village everybody sees everybody and you know that you must work and live a good life. I think the village is like...like a conscience for the people."

Each of these women embodied the "cradle to grave" work ethic handed down from generation to generation. Through apathetic governments as well as oppression, through peace and war, prosperity and poverty, the laboring class had somehow survived. It stung the older peasant women that children were no longer apprentices to their parents in work or in life. Kristina didn't know a lot of things, but she could see easily enough that the flow of youth leaving for the cities was completely changing their village, and their way of life. "Who could blame them, with the temptations of freedom?" she thought silently.

With a cynical smile, Zoya added, "They are looking for what is right under their noses!" Kristina simply nodded her head in agreement.

As they walked along, Kristina recalled the trip that she had taken six years before. That journey had been full of purpose. It meant renewing the paperwork for the small pension she relied on to survive, which meant continued independence rather than working for someone else. It meant time for her to transform the willow branches and reeds from the banks of the river into practical and beautiful objects in her hands. Six years ago, she had left before dawn on a Tuesday. She had walked into the village, where she boarded a rusty, rattling diesel-fueled bus for the two-hour ride to Novnij. The Provincial Records Building there was her destination. Once an almost elegant building, with its white-quarried stone façade, it now wore a coat of soot and grime from nearby coal-fired power plants and wood smoke. The acrid pollution hung in the air from early fall to late spring.

Inside the building, however, it was starkly clean. In a freshly scrubbed corridor, Kristina passed most of the day on a worn mahogany bench. She thought of her parents and how her life mirrored theirs. Neither Dmitri nor Nadia Marchenko had been formally educated, although her father could at least write his name. That was all that was needed then for a peasant farmer; but Kristina's parents made certain that she never missed school. She was a good student and learned quickly. Her skill with numbers won her many certificates of recognition. The Marchenko's life was simple, long and difficult, but the couple was happy and of a single mind in everything. Her mother had never been able to carry another baby and so Kristina remained an only child all her life. She envied those who had brothers and sisters, but accepted that her life was to be alone. The only friend she had was Zoya and her once-a-month conversations with her were welcomed.

It had been no surprise to Kristina that her dear father died less than a month after his wife. She buried them herself, side by side in unmarked graves on a grassy slope overlooking the stone and timber house that Dmitri built. Then, at fifty-eight years of age, Kristina began a solitary life. Alone with her work ethic, her talent for basket weaving and the principle that guided her parents all of their lives: "Be always decent to others and they will be decent to you." Sitting on the mahogany bench in the hall, the only thing on Kristina's mind was Kutzya, who was probably meowing for her at home.

"Marchenkova, Kristina Marchenkova?" a woman's voice echoed Kristina's name off the polished marble floors and walls. "The secretary will see you now."

For the next two hours, Kristina recounted her work life as best as her memory allowed. Through sometimes misty eyes she recalled her teens, twenties and thirties when she still held dreams of a strong, loving man—of a marriage that would never be. When she strayed off the facts, Anya, the brusque young secretary, steered her back quickly. Anya had little patience with this old woman and had heard the story many times from pensioners seeking renewals.

"At least this old woman has her baskets to add to her monthly stipend," she thought, "others are not so fortunate."

With all the honesty she held, Kristina told the woman exactly how many baskets she had sold and their prices. She did not tell her of the long hours it took to make each one, nor of the hours spent collecting the many grasses and branches. She did not mention walking across miles of countryside looking for the perfect shade of bark. Nor did Kristina tell her that her village was a poor village and could not bring the price that baskets would bring in the city. Of course, Kristina had no way of knowing that reporting this additional income would be deducted from her monthly pension. She dutifully reported each one, with the secretary entering the numbers on a sheet of green paper with little boxes.

Determining the basket income was not the primary focus for Anya however. Her interests lay with whether there was anyone else in the home to add to the household support. She continued to press Kristina about a husband. The old woman had long ago become insensitive to this subject. Being a widow would have been acceptable, but her situation seemed peculiar to some people in her culture.

"I have never married and the reasons are many," she said quietly.

It was then that the young stern secretary realized that the woman sitting in front of her had kept her shawl over her head, with one side of her face covered throughout the entire interview. With embarrassment, Anya knew that she had been so absorbed in the function of her job that the people she interviewed often became irrelevant. The barrier that came between the bureaucrat who made life-changing decisions and the pensioners who appealed for increases in their monthly stipend was necessary to shield her feelings of helplessness at their plight.

Anya swallowed hard. "I am so very sorry," she said. "Of course you have your reasons. To be honest, with my husband and his slovenly habits, I sometimes wonder why I *did* get married!"

Her feeble attempt at humor was lost on Kristina, who simply wanted the interview to end. She was tired. It had been a long exhausting day and she still had hours to go before she would be home. She knew Kutzya was meowing loudly, looking for his bowl of warm milk and her lap. Kristina didn't answer, and Anya noticed that the old woman was not going to respond any further.

The interview was over and Kristina left the Provincial Building with its labyrinth of hallways and polished marble floors. She wouldn't know for weeks if her pension was going to be renewed. The wheels turned slowly and "high tech" was an unknown term in this part of the world. Walls of handwritten entries in thick ledger books contained every bit of information on people, but the retrieval process for all this information was rudimentary at best. Attempts at placing the information into computerized form often met with frustration when the electrical supplies were cut and programs were instantly lost. Power surges were constant and computer training was minimal. When a simple glitch that might have been corrected with a few keystrokes occurred, computers were often just covered up and sat unused for months. The old, manual way of record keeping was still preferred by most clerical people. Although Kristina knew that it was easy to fall through the system and become lost in a maze of names and numbers, she also knew that she had done what was required and could do no more than that. It was late in the day and the old woman knew she had to hurry to be on time for the last bus back to the village.

Steel gray clouds blanketed the city in every direction, promising a night of rain and a muddy, pot-holed bus ride home. Kristina walked toward the corner near the bus stop and from out of nowhere, a bicycle appeared. Moving too quickly for Kristina to sidestep him, the young man collided with the old woman. She fell to the pavement, momentarily stunned with pain. The young rider continued on, but not before wrenching the small basket purse from her arm. He left her there, still speechless with pain and confusion.

A few moments later, another stranger helped her to her feet. Kristina quickly grabbed her shawl and wrapped it around her head and face in the habitual gesture produced over the years. She assured the kindly stranger she wasn't hurt and with a shrug of his shoulders, he continued on his way, leaving Kristina with a rip in her only skirt. She brushed off her clothing, and with a heavy heart realized that her bus money was now in the hands of the young ruffian on the bicycle. Replacing her fallen head-scarf, which she retrieved from the sidewalk, she pondered for a moment and then with no other recourse, turned back toward the Provincial Records Building.

After quietly explaining to Anya what had happened, Kristina accepted the few rubles that it would take for her to return to her village before nightfall. Before accepting the money, Kristina, with all the pride she could muster, asked Anya to write the small debt on a piece of paper that she then placed in the pocket of her sweater. The money she was now indebted for paled in comparison to the loss of her dignity in this ordeal.

Anya watched as this proud woman with her mysteriously hidden face once again left her office with her head held high and a slight limp from her fall. "She is a remarkable woman, this Kristina Marchenkova," thought Anya. "It is a pity that something has kept her from a normal life and children to see her through her last years."

Kristina boarded the bus and sat in the rear seat as she always did. Once again, the habit of keeping a low profile was evident in her actions. She pulled her shawl close up and around her face with a practiced motion. Kristina knew that she would probably fall asleep on the long ride home to the village. In doing so, her head-scarf all alone might possibly fall away from her face, exposing the most vulnerable part of this proud peasant woman. In addition, her scarf and shawl provided security from the questioning glances of others and would muffle any sound. She knew she was likely to have dreams that would make her cry out. Those dreams that had haunted her since childhood.

The same frightening scene would often appear in the dreams. Her father, her beloved father, raising his sharp axe to cut wood for the fire; the pretty little blonde girl, standing too close, the sound of a log splitting, sending a sliver of wood deep into the child's left cheek, barely missing an eye, the screams of her mother, the blood everywhere, the fear in her father's eyes and the pain when he pulled the wood from her face. Then, the terror and agonized look on his face as he held her tightly while her mother sewed the split with the coarse cotton thread, tears streaming down her face. The split that later got infected and required poultices of herbs and left the jagged scar that changed her life.

This single moment in time would condemn her to her solitary life. It had taken months to heal the gaping wound. Fevers and knives cutting away rotted flesh were unbearable. School was out of the question afterwards, with jeering and shouts of "Monster" echoing in the forest. Her parents, out of both guilt and protection kept her hidden away from the prying eyes of the villagers for months at a time. She had become used to the loneliness. Kristina sat in the back of the bus and slept soundly, her head-scarf wrapped tightly around her face for the entire journey home to safety. She never again returned to the city, but paid her debt through another traveler within the month.

Walking in the village with Zoya was not *always* a pleasant experience for Kristina. Zoya spoke to everyone they passed, chattering all the time. She knew everything about everyone else in the village and picked up small bits of gossip as they sauntered. Fifteen-year-old Natalia remained the topic through the morning between the two women as they discussed the changing morality of the times. It was an age-old conversation, repeated all over the world, but these women were unaware of circumstances beyond the boundaries of their local area. They made their way through a village that had gone unchanged for centuries. Department stores and traffic lights were beyond their comprehension. The tiny village, with its cobblestone streets and wooden storefronts, symbolized the lives of its residents, simple and unassuming, and personal lives became the focus of its interests. Friendships were forged on the fires of trust and broken with betrayal. Relationships, as well as animosities, were carried on through generations. Such was the case with a storekeeper who was dishonest. No one could remember *exactly* when Nikolai Shtrykov's grandfather had cheated his customers, but two generations later, the reputation of his fabric shop still suffered. His grandson, also Nikolai, barely scratched out a living while trying to repair the damage of two generations ago. Zoya and Kristina passed Nikolai's fabric shop without a glance and arrived at the last row of shops they would visit.

Separately bargaining for apples and dried berries, Kristina indulged herself with a small amount of butter for the two loaves of black bread she purchased. The basket she carried held less than its capacity, but it would be a long walk home and she knew better than to weight it too heavily. They turned the corner and with sighs of relief saw the long red painted bench in front of Evgeny's shop. This would be their last stop of the day, as usual. The welcoming smell of Turkish coffee beans and an assortment of teas drifted out of the open doorway as they entered.

White-bearded Evgeny greeted them warmly, "So, how are the two most beautiful women in town today?" His resounding voice and twinkling eyes made both women blush, despite his obvious mischievous comment.

Evgeny Gargarin loved life—it was that simple. He was never seen with a frown on his face or a crease in his forehead from worry. A devoutly religious man, his shop had a corner altar with icons of many saints and plastic flowers displayed prominently. His patrons would often find him deep in prayer when they entered the shop and learned to wait patiently for him to finish his melodious chants.

His love for all of life extended to animals as well. Evgeny had a collection of animals that seemed, almost deliberately, to seek his help. Injured birds, rodents and sometimes even farm animals could always be found tied or caged in back of the shop, ready for release when they recovered. Today, Evgeny had a small canary in a cage with a light bulb shining in on it. A tattered cotton towel covered most of the cage.

Evgeny explained, "I think he has a slight cold, so I gave him some herb tea. He will be fine and singing again soon."

The rumor was widely spread that "Old Evgeny could even speak to the animals and they understand him." It was true that when Evgeny spoke to his little visitors, he would use a strange language of noises. Clicks, whistles and soft whispers, intermingled with little chuckles and sometimes amused laughter, would provoke an interchange with the critters. On the rare occasion when an animal was beyond his help, Evgeny would sometimes stay by its side until it breathed its last breath. Afterward, he would place it in a small box, with exquisite painted crosses of his Orthodox faith on the lid. Solemnly he would carry the container to the large area behind the shop where he had created a rather large cemetery. From time to time, there would be objections from neighboring shopkeepers, but everyone loved Evgeny and their complaints soon subsided.

Evgeny's only son, Ilya, was usually in the shop, often in the corner or sweeping the sidewalk outside. Today, Ilya sat quietly painting in the corner. From the time he was a small child, his drawings and colorings were done from this corner. Sometimes he painted the customers as they stood choosing coffee beans at the old wooden counter. Sometimes he painted his father as he stood at the altar praying. Today he was painting an intricate design on the lid of a small wooden box that was waiting for the next lifeless creature that would need a final resting place.

Ilya rarely spoke to the customers in his father's shop. In fact, Ilya hardly ever spoke at all. He had been born "slow" to learn more than the basics of life. Ilya could not calculate numbers, nor could he tell time very well. He learned to sign his name, but this took years of patient diligence by Evgeny to accomplish. His father's love shielded him from the taunts of other children, and with his protective actions, Evgeny kept the boy out of school for most of his life.

Everyone knew that Evgeny's wife had died along with a baby daughter many years ago, leaving Ilya and his father to live alone. Always talking and with an enthusiasm that was contagious to his customers, the subject of his son was the only thing that would cause Evgeny's smile to fade. He worried often about the future of his man/child son. Knowing that Ilya would never be able to take over the duties of the coffee shop and possessing no other skills to produce an income was the subject of most of Evgeny's prayers. He trusted God completely. However, he also knew that he had to do *his* part to help.

Zoya and Kristina listened to the little chirps of the small bird and Zoya said teasingly, "I see that you have another creature to care for, *Doktor* Gargarin. Did you put some new magic herb in its tea to make it sing in the voice of a frog? Or perhaps it was a frog and now it is a bird?"

They all laughed, even Ilya in his corner laughed in the simple camaraderie they all felt. Kristina stood behind her large friend as she often did, unconsciously pulling her head-scarf further over her left cheek. The motion did not go unnoticed by Evgeny. He felt the sting of her embarrassment and shame from the quiet woman who was hiding part of herself from the world.

"All right, Evgeny," Zoya asked, "how many rubles are you going to steal from us today for your coffee beans? Every time we come in, the prices seem to go up higher and higher."

She laughed with him as he moved toward the bins of coffee beans and responded, "But, Zoya, I only raise the prices when I see you coming down the street." He looked at Kristina and thought he saw a slight smile lift the corners of her mouth. He was satisfied. Making people smile was his triumph over the sadness of life.

Evgeny knew what had happened to Kristina as a child. Everyone in the little village knew the story of the little girl with the terrible scar from a woodcutting incident so many years ago. There were many such scars on the villagers, but none inflicted by parents, as was Kristina's. The missing limbs and scars of torture and war were common, but borne by those who suffered at the hands of enemies. Evgeny was once one of the young children who teased her and called her terrible names all those years ago. He wanted many times to tell her how sorry he was. He had carried the regrets of being a young bully as his cross to bear each time he saw her. However, he could never find her alone and certainly did not want to embarrass her further in front of her friend. He was happy that she even came into his store, giving him the occasional opportunity to be nice to her from time to time.

Kristina had no way of knowing that he felt such remorse after so many years. She had been made fun of by so many when she was a child, she could not remember who it was who said things to her and who had not. All she felt now was kindness and warmth from this man and she appreciated how he always made her smile. Although Zoya was her friend, she seldom gave Kristina reason to smile, at least not in the warm way that Evgeny did.

Kristina shyly smiled until Zoya suddenly walked across the room toward the bins of candy, leaving Kristina standing alone with Evgeny. It was an awkward moment for both of them without the buffer of Zoya's easy conversation. Kristina was at a loss for words when she suddenly remembered the canary. "I hope he feels better very soon," she said timidly, nodding her head toward the small bird.

"He will recover, I am sure, and will sing his praises to the sky as before," assured Evgeny, with a nod of his thick white head. He suddenly had an idea and asked, "But I would appreciate your help for a moment before you leave."

Kristina looked bewildered, but answered politely, "Of course—what can I do to help?"

"If you would just hold him while I give him some more peppermint tea, he might take more than I could give him with only one hand."

"I have held many birds in the forest when they fell from their nests," said Kristina, "certainly I will help."

Evgeny reached into the cage and gently placed the bird in Kristina's hands. She cradled it tenderly. Evgeny took a small piece of cloth and dipped a corner of it into a sweet-smelling concoction in a small cup next to the cage. He squeezed the cloth into the bird's beak while Kristina watched, her head bent low. Making little clicking sounds with his tongue, Evgeny did not notice Kristina's head-scarf shifting away from her cheek. Kristina, however, did feel the movement, but with both hands holding the tiny creature, there was nothing she could do about it. The scarf slipped further and as the ends loosened, it exposed the scar that had been hidden so carefully for so long. Kristina froze momentarily, and caught her breath. The sharp intake causing Evgeny to look up. Like a frightened animal, she looked at him with pleading in her eyes.

Sensing her appeal for help, Evgeny Gargarin did what Kristina would never have allowed a living soul to do. He reached up and removed her head-scarf completely, draping it over her shoulder. Softly he said, "There now, such beauty should not be hidden a moment longer."

The bird moved in her hands and Evgeny opened the door of the cage, signaling Kristina to place it back inside. Zoya was moving toward them and it was evident that she was ready to leave. With both hands now free, Kristina quickly replaced the old faded floral head-scarf and tied it securely.

Returning home, Kristina's life resumed its normal routine. Rising before dawn, coaxing the embers of the small fire to life, fixing her breakfast of tea and black bread spread with a tiny amount of butter, followed by an hour of chopping wood. A short rest and then an early morning walk to gather the treasures from the forest floor. The bounty consisted of twigs, bark, moss and branches of willow and other trees, supple enough to twist and curve while maintaining their strength without splitting. The rippling sound of the river a few meters away promised rushes and reeds that were useful as well.

The river was where Kristina would rest on her "thinking bench," a half-sawn log that had been placed across two tree stumps by her father many years ago. Over the years, the vegetation had grown thick and surrounded the natural bench, only steps away from the riverbank. It was a haven of natural beauty where the outside world seemed a million miles away. Squirrels and other small creatures scampered through a cleared area in front of the bench and often watched the old woman with great interest.

She had been coming to this spot since she was a small child. Sometimes to watch her father fishing in the river and sometimes just to sit and reflect, without the scarf on her head. Kristina frequently ate her lunch while sitting on the "thinking bench," allowing herself time enough to rest before resuming her search for materials. The slight chill in the air and the thickness of the squirrels' tails foretold a hard winter ahead, she noted. She relaxed and took a deep breath of the forest air.

It was only here that she felt truly safe and where she had made her first basket using the rushes and reeds near the river. Her father had gone upriver to fish and when he returned and saw that first little basket, he almost burst with pride and amazement. The colors and the design were unlike anything he had seen before. Of course his wife made baskets, as most peasant women did. They were simple, but strong and practical. It was a skill that his wife's family had passed on and now his little girl was learning. But, this, this was a work of art! It was a tiny basket, but he proudly brought it home and set it in a special place on the wardrobe closet. He began to encourage her to make many more and began taking them to the village market. Through the years, the extra money had helped them over many hard times.

On this beautiful autumn day, Kristina sat and relived the day in Evgeny's shop. "He used the word *beauty* for me," she thought. "No one but my parents ever said I was a *beauty!* Such nonsense talk!" she said under her breath. She tried to dismiss his comment, but felt her face flushing, and not with her usual embarrassment.

The weather was perfect for a collecting day and Kristina got up from her bench and began her walk along the river. She would fill the hours humming folk songs of her childhood and gathering works of art from Nature's bosom. On this late September day, Kristina's thoughts were of much more than reeds and rushes. Alone and unseen, without the headscarf and with trembling fingers, she touched her left cheek. The jagged scar was still there, but under her fingers, her face felt much more damaged. "No one could think this a beautiful face," she thought sadly.

Returning to her tiny one-room home, Kristina emptied the contents of her collecting basket in the middle of the plank table to be sorted. She was startled by a heavy knock at the door. Standing in the doorway was the smiling Evgeny. Behind him was Ilya, silently holding something covered with a heavy cloth. "May we come in?" asked Evgeny.

Kristina stepped aside, and offered the only chair in her little home to Evgeny, who sat down and then patted his leg for Kutzya, who immediately jumped into his lap. Ilya placed the object he was holding on the plank table and uncovered it.

"It's the little canary!" exclaimed Kristina.

"Yes, you helped to make him better and he told me he would like for you to own him," said Evgeny with a big smile. He added, "He will sing when the sun is up and you will hear that his voice is once again beautiful and sounds nothing like a frog." They all laughed at the remark, Ilya laughed loudly and began to make frog noises. Evgeny then addressed Kutzya and said, "And you, old man cat, will you promise to become friends with your new little friend?" Kutzya opened one eye lazily and meowed in response.

No one noticed that Ilya had moved to the shelf of baskets. He picked one up and was examining it closely. Ilya selected and separated a total of six baskets before Kristina was aware of his actions. Nodding toward him, she said to Evgeny, "It looks as if Ilya has found something that interests him." She went to the pile of straw and twigs and handed some to Ilya.

"This is the way they begin." Ilya looked at the twigs in his hands and smiled in amazement.

"How this become that?" he said, pointing to the baskets.

"Someday, I will show you how to do it, with your father's permission," replied Kristina.

"Yes, of course, you have my permission, but right now we must leave, son," said Evgeny. "We have to be home before dark and the sun is almost gone to bed," he added, almost apologetically.

It was long after Evgeny and Ilya were gone from sight when Kristina reached up to pull her scarf over her cheek. She was shocked to find that it was gone. In a panic, she saw it lying on the rocker where Evgeny had been sitting. Kristina realized that she had not felt self-conscious at all in front of Evgeny, nor did he stare at her face for a moment. All the years of protecting herself seemed suddenly to disappear. For the first time since the accident, Kristina felt accepted. She walked to the old rocker, picked up the sleeping Kutzya and placed him in her lap as she sat down. Crying slow, hot tears, Kristina fell asleep listening to the soft peeping of the canary as it settled itself for the night.

The weeks seemed to fly by and it was time again for the next trip to the village. This time it was for much larger purchases. Setting in the extra supplies for winter was a difficult task; but lamp oil, yarn and bags of flour were necessary to survive it.

Kristina felt butterflies in her stomach as she prepared the wooden wagon that would take her baskets and return with a heavier load of winter goods. Her anxiety was not from the hope of bartering the baskets, it sprang from the inner strength that only dignity can supply.

She was not going to wear the old floral head-scarf.

Beginning with the night of Evgeny and Ilya's visit, each day Kristina wore it less and less. She had done her chores without it, she had left it behind when gathering basket materials and had gotten used to seeing her reflection in the dirty glass of the windowpane without it. Now came the biggest test of all. Today, she would not wear it to the village. At the last minute, trying to decide whether to stuff it in the pocket of her gray sweater, she took it and spread it out on the seat of the old rocker. Taking a big breath, Kristina Marchenko closed the door firmly and took up the long wooden handle of the wagon.

Zoya, as usual, was sitting on the wall of the fountain waiting for her. As usual, she stood up and waved when she saw Kristina coming toward her. As Kristina approached, however, Zoya's hand stopped waving. Her hand stayed motionless in the air as her old friend drew closer. Zoya was speechless at seeing the thick white hair without a covering. She hugged Kristina as usual, but did not mention the scarf. Zoya took special care not to stare at the jagged scar, but took sidelong glances as they walked.

Kristina seemed comfortable though, and Zoya noticed a remarkable change in their discussion. Kristina was animated and kept up a constant stream of chatter. No longer reticent and content with being the listener, she smiled easily and kept the flow of conversation moving. Zoya was astounded at the change in her friend, but respected her and would not ask what caused it, despite her curiosity.

Kristina grew quiet as they approached the square however. For a moment, she almost reached into her sweater pocket for the scarf and then realized she had not brought it with her. She swallowed hard and straightened her back. Proudly, she walked next to Zoya, pulling the wagon behind her. The women bargained with shopkeepers and Kristina traded two baskets for a bag of flour and three more baskets for a large container of cooking oil. Her best baskets, those made to be used for decorations, were traded for some salted meat. It took most of the morning to bargain with the shopkeepers, but Kristina was intent on her task and did not notice anyone staring at her face. Zoya helped her to place the paper-wrapped bundle of meat in the wagon, and the women knew it was time to head for the last row of shops before returning home.

"I wonder what animals are at *Doktor* Gargarin's shop today?" mused Zoya.

Kristina was silent and seemed to slow her steps as they approached the long red bench outside. The door to Evgeny's shop stood wide open as the women entered. Seeing him at the altar, they quietly stood and waited. Ilya was in the corner with a large pad of drawing paper. He was looking from the paper to his father and seemed lost in thought as he sketched. Standing in front of the altar, Evgeny was praying the ancient prayer of Optina Pustyn, a monastery in the northern part of Russia. His deep voice resonated the words:

> *God, please let me meet with calm to my soul all that the coming day will bring me.*
>
> *God, I pass myself to Your sacred will.*
>
> *God, in every hour of this day help me and show me the way.*
>
> *God, teach me to meet all the news that I get during this day with a quiet soul and strong belief that it is Your sacred will.*
>
> *God, guide my words and deeds and feelings. In any unforeseen event, do not let me forget that it is Your sacred will.*
>
> *God, teach me to deal correctly and reasonably with every member of my family, without causing confusion and distress to anybody.*
>
> *God, give me the strength to live through the pressures of the coming days and through its events. Guide my will and teach me how to pray, believe, hope, have patience, forgive and love. Amen.*

His head bowed, and as he finished his prayer he made the sign of the cross from his forehead, and then to each shoulder, slowly and deliberately. The he let out a long sigh. He blew out the candle on the altar and turned, seeing Kristina and Zoya. "And how are the two most beautiful women in the village today?" he said, smiling broadly.

Evgeny immediately noticed the missing head-scarf and his eyes opened wide. However, as Zoya had done, he remained silent. He felt his heart beating faster as he tried to remain calm. "Look, Ilya, look who is here. It is the new guardian of the little canary! And how is the voice of our little friend today?" he asked.

"She is doing quite well," answered Kristina. "You may come and visit her anytime if you like." The words were out of her mouth before she could stop them and she blushed with embarrassment.

Ilya left his corner, carrying his drawing pad. Standing next to his father, the boy hesitantly handed the oversized tablet to Kristina.

"I, I, m-made this, it is for y-you," he stammered.

Looking down at the book, Kristina gasped, "It is beautiful, Ilya! You have made a perfect picture of the baskets!" Zoya and Evgeny looked over her shoulder at an exact image of the shelf in Kristina's home that held her finished baskets. Every tiny detail of the reeds and straw had been drawn with precision. It was almost photographic in its quality.

Ilya beamed with the praises of the three adults and then turned the page of the book. "I made another one t-too."

The next picture was startling as well. It was a perfect likeness of Kristina! A perfect likeness, with one exception her cheeks were both as smooth as glass. There was not a trace of the scar in his portrayal of her.

Seeing her instinctively reach for her left cheek, Evgeny reached out and took her wrist gently. "He sees your beauty as all those who love you see it," he said.

With tear-filled eyes, Kristina swallowed hard and whispered, "Thank you for helping me to see myself." Looking out at the fading light and her overflowing wagon, she said, "Zoya, we must hurry, it is getting late."

"Ilya," Evgeny quickly said, "that wagon looks very heavy, please help Madame Marchenkova to take it home. Then, come back along the road the same way as soon as you are finished helping to unload her things." Kristina started to protest, but Evgeny firmly said, "He needs the fresh air, he has been sitting and drawing all day long."

Zoya went her own way home at the crossroad by the fountain. She hugged Kristina, promising to be at their meeting place the following month if the weather permitted. Ilya and Kristina walked the rest of the way home, with Kristina pointing out all the differences in the bark on the trees and the various grasses along the way. Ilya listened with great attention to her as he pulled the wagon behind him. His indoor pastime of painting and drawing had not allowed time for outdoor interests. His father's shop kept him indoors most of the time, and as the young man listened, he discovered a whole world of nature's wonders to be explored and appreciated.

Their arrival at Kristina's home awakened old Kutzya from his nap. The canary was trilling as they approached and the tranquility of the little cottage beckoned them. Ilya helped carry the sacks of flour and oil to the storage area. He hung the salted meat high on a hook in a little shed attached to the back of the house and covered it with a burlap bag. When he finished, he put the wagon behind the house and covered it with a large black canvas. Coming to the door to say good-bye to Kristina, Ilya stood quietly watching his new friend. Kristina had gathered some material for baskets on the walk back and wasted no time preparing them for later use. Ilya watched as she worked the long pump handle until the spout coughed up splashes of water. She filled the waiting pan in the wooden tub that was her sink.

"Would you like to help, Ilya?" she asked. He quickly nodded his agreement. At her request, Ilya handed her a fistful of willow branches, which she curled and left to soak. Taking a small dried limb, with amazing dexterity, Kristina peeled strips of bark from it and then set it aside. Ilya tried the same technique, but the limb snapped. His look of surprise made Kristina laugh as she handed him another one.

"Take your time Ilya," she said gently, "there is no hurry in this work and no right or wrong. You must only know the personality of the material you are working with."

With surprise, Ilya responded, "That is what my father says about the animals. Each one has a different personality. It is like my pencils and my paints. They have different personalities also."

Kristina smiled at the comparisons. It was time for Ilya to leave, but not before promising Kristina that he would return to watch her and learn the making of a basket.

True to his word, the next week saw Ilya return to the little house in the forest. Accompanying him was his father, bringing two dozen eggs as a gift and some coffee beans. Evgeny also brought some nails and a hammer, hard to come by items these days, and set about making some small repairs on the house. Meanwhile, Ilya went inside to be with Kristina.

Using a variety of twigs that had been soaked to make them pliable, Kristina worked them with her fingers, weaving them together in a lattice pattern. Soon Ilya was imitating her. Although somewhat clumsy in his first efforts, his sensitive fingers soon learned to make a tight lattice pattern. The base was soon finished, with longer willows standing vertically. One by one, strands of various shades of twigs and willow branches were worked in and out of the vertical willows until they formed the shell of the basket. Ilya was no longer taking direction from Kristina. Once he understood the basics of making the basket strong and holding weaving tight, his young nimble fingers and his artistic vision took over. His eyes sparkled and he bit his lip as he began to see the endless possibilities before him. He especially liked that there was no right or wrong in designing each piece. In this at least, his peers could not judge him.

Fridays became a special time for Evgeny and his son. They would close the shop early and walk through the forest to Kristina's. From there, they would comb the surrounding area for basket-making material. Knowing there were only a few weeks left till the first snowfall buried nature's treasures made the forest treks necessary as well as fun. The scavengers, under Kristina's tutelage, were very selective and spent hours looking for the hard-to-find tall grasses found only by the river. Kristina introduced Evgeny and Ilya to her "thinking bench," and one important day found the two adults taking a rest before joining Ilya, who was down at the riverbank.

Watching him, Evgeny said, "My son has never been happier, Kristina." He had become familiar with holding her hand over the past few weeks and now, still holding her right hand, he dropped to one knee. "I love you with all my heart," he said softly, "and I would consider it an honor if you were to agree to be my wife."

Kristina said, "I never thought I could so completely trust my heart to someone, but I trust and respect you, Evgeny." With an overflow of emotion, she said, "Yes, of course I will be your wife, and proudly so."

Ilya came up from the riverbank, holding the remains of the season's long grasses. He was carrying one of his own baskets, a creation of his first labors at this new craft. It resembled a bird's nest and Ilya had adopted it as his own, used only for collecting bits of bark and fallen cones. He smiled when Evgeny told him the news and said, "Now you can teach me all day and all night how to make more baskets!"

Both Evgeny and Kristina laughed. Kristina hugged Ilya, saying, "Yes, Ilya, I will spend all my waking hours helping you, but you must promise me that they will be your designs and not always my old ones. The baskets need new life and your vision to continue."

They returned to the tiny house and after dinner, Ilya began to finish a basket he had been working on for the past three weeks while Evgeny and Kristina made plans for the future. While they talked, the boy worked patiently, but with determination. He bit his lower lip; occasionally lifting the basket up in the air to gain a better perspective. Unlike the small bird's nests of his first efforts, this basket characterized his patience. It was grand and dignified. The flat bottom ballooned into round walls. Row upon row of willows, twenty-one in all, were laced in and around nine spines with just a whisper of air between the rows. Abruptly, about half-way up, Ilya allowed the basket to take a deep breath, using only seven more bands of assorted reeds to reach the lip. At midpoint, to dramatize the coming airiness, he selected increasingly lighter colors of the willow branches to contrast the rich tones of the lower portion. Finished, the basket showed a unique uplifting quality.

Evgeny was helping Kristina with the after-dinner cleaning up when silence made him look over to the corner. Seeing Ilya sleeping on the floor, curled up with a blanket, with Kutzya loudly purring next to him, and the new basket on the shelf above his head, Evgeny's heart brimmed with gratitude. His son had learned a craft that would last a lifetime. Evgeny turned to Kristina and said, "You have given me gifts more valuable than gold."

Kristina was puzzled. She thought for a moment and questioned, "But Evgeny, *I* am the one who has received the valuable gifts."

Ilya, awakened by their voices, sleepily said, "I think all gifts should come in a basket."

*   *   *

The Gargarin family is happy and well. Kutzya and the canary coexist, albeit carefully. Gargarin baskets are now sold through distributors in the big cities of the region. Kristina still advises Ilya on their construction, while Ilya uses his own skill and imagination to design baskets of all types.

Evgeny handles the business end of things, and has hired Zoya to run the coffee shop. The entire family now uses the tiny one-room house in the forest as their home and often go to the "thinking bench" to sit and discuss life.

Kristina still has the floral head-scarf, but it is now in a trunk in the pocket of an old gray sweater.

Printed in the United States
946800009B